# Idalia

# Idalia

## Or, The Unfortunate Mistress

# Eliza Haywood

MINT EDITIONS

*Idalia: Or, The Unfortunate Mistress* was first published in 1723.

This edition published by Mint Editions 2021.

ISBN 9781513291581 | E-ISBN 9781513294438

Published by Mint Editions®

MINT
EDITIONS

minteditionbooks.com

Publishing Director: Jennifer Newens
Design & Production: Rachel Lopez Metzger
Project Manager: Micaela Clark
Typesetting: Westchester Publishing Services

# Contents

# Part I

If there were a Possibility that the Warmth and Vigour of Youth cou'd be temper'd with a due Consideration, and the Power of judging rightly, how easy were it to avoid the Ills which most of us endure? How few would be unhappy? With what Serenity might the *Noon* of Life glide on, could we account with Reason for our *Morning* Actions! We hear, indeed, daily Complaints of the Cruelty of *Fate;* but if we examine the Source, we shall find almost all the Woes we languish under are self-caus'd; and that either to pursue the Gratification of some unruly Passion, or shun the Performance of an incumbent Duty, those Misfortunes which so fill the World derive their Being and would more justly merit *Condemnation* than *Compassion*, were not the Fault too universal.

Don *Bernardo de Bellsache*, a Nobleman of *Venice*, had a Daughter whom he esteem'd the Blessing of his Age; and had her Conduct been such as might have been expected from the Elegance of her Genius, and the Improvements of Education, which his Fondness had indulg'd her in, she had indeed been the Wonder of her Sex. Imagination cannot form a Face more exquisitely lovely; such Majesty, such Sweetness, such a Regularity in all her Features, accompany'd with an Air at once so soft, so striking, that while she *commanded* she *allur'd*, and *forc'd* what she *entreated.* Nor was her Shape and Mien less worthy Admiration; it was impossible for anything to be more exactly proportion'd than the *former;* and for the *latter*, it had a Grace peculiar to itself: The least and most careless Motion of her Head or Hand, was sufficient to captivate a Heart. In fine, her Charms were so infinitely above Description, that it was necessary to see her, to have any just Notion of her.—But, alas! to what End serv'd all this Beauty, these uncommon Qualifications, but to make her more remarkably unhappy? She had a *Wit*, which gain'd her no fewer Adorers than her other Perfections; yet not enough to defend her from the Assaults of almost every Passion human Nature is liable to fall into. The Greatness of her Spirit (which from her Childhood had been untameable, or was render'd so thro' the too-great indulgence of her doating Parents) made her unable to endure Controul, disdainful of Advice, obstinate, and peremptory in following her own *Will* to what Extremes soever it led her: The Consequence of such a Disposition could not be expected to be very fortunate, but it brought on her such dreadful Inconveniencies, as all who find in themselves the least Propensity to be of such a Humour, ought to tremble at the Repetition of, and exert their utmost Reason to extirpate.

*Idalia* (for that was the Name of this lovely Inconsiderate) had no sooner arriv'd at her fourteenth Year, than she attracted the Eyes of all the young Noblemen of *Venice;* scarce a Heart but sigh'd for her: The Shrine of our *Blessed Lady* of *Loretto* was never throng'd with greater Numbers of *Religious Devotees* than Don *Bernardo's* House was by those of the Young and Gay; and happy did they think themselves, whose Birth or Fortune gave them any just Cause to hope the Pretensions they brought would be an Offering worth Acceptance. There were some too, (as no Climate is barren of *Fops*) who had the Vanity, without either of these Advantages, to promise themselves Success; of this last Number was *Florez*, one, who, if he had not been possess'd with more Assurance than is ordinarily to be found even among the most Tenacious, would not have presumed, tho' his Passion had been really as violent as he endeavour'd to make it appear, to have declared it. He was descended from a Family, in which there never had been one whose Actions had entitled him to bear Arms; the Height of his Parent's Ambition had been to prefer him, when a Child, to be Page to Don *Ferdinand*, Nephew to the *Doge*. With this young Nobleman he had travell'd; and all the Education he was Master of was owing to this Advantage, as was the Post he possess'd in the Army, to his Favour: For being naturally of a designing sordid Disposition, by falling in with all his Humours, promoting his Pleasures, and flattering his Vices, he had wound himself so much into the good Will of his Lord, that he refused him nothing. The Intimacy with which he was treated by so great a Man, and the sudden Elevation of his Fortune, join'd to some fulsome Praises of his Beauty, and fine Wit, which those Women, who are paid for their Favours, generally lavish on the Person who makes Choice of them, gave him so good an Opinion of his own Merit, that he thought it an Impossibility for any Woman to be insensible of it; and look'd on the Attainment of *Idalia*, notwithstanding the Multitude of her Admirers, and the vast Possessions she was likely to be Mistress of, as a Thing not at all difficult.

But whatever he imagin'd to himself, *Bernardo* had Sentiments quite different from these: He had no sooner discover'd his Design, than he forbad him his House in Terms which sufficiently told him he was in Earnest, and chid his Daughter for entertaining a Proposal so unsuitable to her Birth, with more Sharpness than the Manner in which he had ever behaved to her, could give her Leave to think was in his Nature: But as the Vanity and unthinking Pride which sway'd the Actions of this young Lady had shew'd itself in the encouraging all who pretended to admire her, of what Degree soever they were, so now the Obstinacy of her Humour began to appear, in the Uneasiness she felt at her Father's Commands, never to see *Florez* more. Amidst the Multiplicity of her Adorers, she thought herself undone to miss the Addresses of a single Votary, and could not bear to lose the Conversation of a Man whose Eyes and Tongue were perfectly skill'd in the Art of Flattery and Dissimulation, and had given her so many Informations of her Power. And wholly leaving herself to the Dictates of her Impatience, grew almost distracted to think she was debarr'd the Enjoyment of anything she found a Pleasure in. She began immediately to lessen her Regard for her too-long indulgent Father, which by degrees ripen'd to a Contempt of him, and ended in a Resolution to act in everything according to her Inclinations, without giving herself any Pain how far it would be consonant to his.

In this ruinous Disposition it came into her Head to write to *Florez*; not that she was really in *love* with him, or had yet any Notion of that Passion; but *Vanity*, that reigning Faculty of her Soul, prompted her to use her utmost Efforts for the retrieving a Heart she began to fear was estranged. And indeed, this Conjecture was not in the least unreasonable; for, had he, in Sincerity, been so entirely devoted to her as he had once endeavour'd to perswade her he was, *Love*, always fruitful in Invention, would have furnish'd him with some Stratagem, either to have seen her, or convey'd a Letter to her; for some Weeks had pass'd between the Time of his being forbid his Visits, and that in which she writ. She did not fail to upbraid him with his Coldness; but withal let him know she had good Nature enough to pardon it; desired an Answer; and that for the future, if she was really happy enough to retain any Place in his Remembrance, he would let no Day escape without giving her some Assurances of it. In short, no Woman, who felt the severest Pangs of desperate dying Love, could write more passionately, or express a greater Concern at being abandon'd by the Man her Soul was fond of, than what the Spirit of *Coquetry* taught the Pen of the inconsiderate *Idalia*. She concluded her Epistle with a hearty Wish, *Grant Heaven!* (said she to herself,) *that I may once more have him in my Power to use him as I please, let the Consequence be what it will.* She bribed a Servant to deliver it, and bring and Answer back: But the Uneasiness she was in till the Return of her Messenger was such, as whoever had been witness of, could not have imagin'd to have sprung from any other Source than Love. But to such a Degree does the immoderate Love of Praise transport some People, that to lose any Opportunity of receiving it, is a Torment equal to that which others feel in a Disappointment of the most essential Blessings.

The Return of her Emissary brought but little Ease to the Suspence she had endur'd while he was gone: *Florez*, indeed, had sent by him; but his Letter appear'd so different from those she had formerly receiv'd from him, that the Hand was all that shew'd 'em writ by the same Person. A Penetration like her's could easily discern the Alteration; she found the Style was forc'd, formal, and affected; and where he said he still continu'd to adore her, and should never cease to do so, it was in such a Manner as plainly shew'd his Heart had no Part in dictating such Expressions. And, in truth, never Woman was more disappointed in her Aim, that was this Lady: In spite of the Attractions she was Mistress of, *Florez* had either an Insensibility of them, or had Resolution enough to withstand the Emotions of his Tenderness, whenever he found 'em contrary to his Interest. 'Tis probable, by what after ensu'd, that a Daughter of Don *Bernardo's*, tho' never so disagreeable, would have had Charms sufficient to have retain'd his Adorations; but *Idalia*, all lovely as she was, without the Addition of that Fortune her Father's Consent must give, had no longer any Charms to hold him.

'Tis easy to imagine it was no small Shock to her Pride, to find the Advances she had made were receiv'd with no more Warmth: But suffering all Consideration to be wholly drown'd in the o'erflowing Folly which at present possess'd her, she continued daily by Letters to give him Occasion to believe there was nothing on Earth so desirable as his Conversation; and that it was not impossible she might be prevail'd on to become his Wife, tho' by it she should lose a Father. But there was not the least Pressure in any of his Answers, which testified he wish'd she should run so great a Risque. This so nettled her, that at last, 'tis probable, she would have look'd upon him, as indeed he was, a Conquest far unworthy of the Pains she had taken. She was just beginning to give over all Thoughts of him, when her ill Fate, taking the Advantage of the *Baseness* of his Nature, and the unaccountable *Fantastickness* of her's, gave a sudden Turn to this Adventure, which was to terminate in her utter Undoing.

If there can be anything to be alledg'd in the Defence of Vanity, the fair *Idalia*, on the Account of her Youth, her Beauty, Birth, and Fortune, had certainly more to plead in her Behalf, than where there were none of these Advantages: *Florez*, who had nothing distinguishably valuable either in his Person or Accomplishments, and was of a Sex in which that *Foible* is far less excusable than in the weaker, had yet as large a Share: He could not imagine himself belov'd by a Woman so admired by all the World, without communicating the Secret. To those *Insensibles* all the Pleasure of an *Amour* consists in the *Reputation* of it: To be *accounted well* in the Esteem of a Person of *ordinary* Qualifications, yields them infinitely more Satisfaction than the *real Enjoyment* of one of the most *Excellent* could do. It is not therefore to be wonder'd at, that a Man, who had neither Love nor Honour to restrain him, triumph'd in an Affair like this: He could not hear the Charms of *Idalia* mention'd, without letting the Company know how much it was in his Power to become Master of them; and to prove the Truth of what he said, expos'd her Letters, those fatal and undisputable Testimonials of her Folly. Few that had any Acquaintance with him, were Strangers to his Happiness; but none more envy'd his good Fortune than his Patron Don *Ferdinand*. This young Lord was of a Disposition exceeding amorous: He long had view'd *Idalia* with those Desires which it was common for her to inspire; but finding in himself not the least Propensity to Marriage, and believing it impossible to obtain her by any other Means, had endeavour'd to stifle the hopeless Passion by other Amusements; till hearing the Condescensions she had made to one whom he had so much Power over, he immediately had it in his Thoughts to make use of it for the Gratification of his Wishes. There needed but little Ceremony in the communicating his Design to a Person so much his Creature; nor durst *Florez*, if he had had an Inclination, oppose what he required; but on the contrary, he was glad of an Opportunity of serving him in a Manner which would so considerably advance his Interest with him. It was presently agreed between them, that he, the favour'd Lover, should write to *Idalia* in the most passionate and moving strain imaginable, assuring her, That nothing was so insupportable as the Pangs of Absence; that he died to see her; and intreat her to grant him that Favour at the House of a particular Friend, whom he mention'd in the Letter, and gave her Directions how to find it. This Epistle being dictated by the impatient Wishes of the amorous *Ferdinand*, had infinitely more Force of Perswasion in it, than anything the Insensible *Florez* could have said without his Assistance; and they both promised themselves it would succeed as they would have it, to engage her to come to the Place appointed for the Assignation; which was a House where they had frequently rioted in those dissolute Enjoyments Youth is too prone to be fond of, and the People who liv'd in it entirely at the Devotion of Don *Ferdinand*.

By this cursed Contrivance was the rash unthinking *Idalia* betray'd: She receiv'd the fraudulent Mandate, swallow'd the well-dress'd artful Flattery it contain'd with a prodigious deal of Pleasure, and return'd an Answer of Consent. Not that she was without a Thought at the Liberty he took in naming a Place of Assignation, since it had been much more agreeable to the *Venetian* Address, to have watch'd her coming out, follow'd her to Church, or any other publick Place, and at an humble Distance gaz'd upon her: But she imputed his Boldness to the Violence of his Passion; and having no other Design than to make him the Slave of her Beauty, resolv'd to see him, the better to secure her Conquest, and punish him *hereafter* by her Contempt and Coldness, for his *present* Presumption.

Adorn'd, and every Charm illustrated with all the Aids of Art, assur'd of Victory, and already exulting with a prideful Scorn for the Triumphs of her Eyes, she set out, under the Pretence of going to *Vespers*, attended only by one Servant; whom she sent back immediately to fetch her *Beads*, which she told him she had forgot; and as soon as she saw herself at Liberty, turn'd another way, and went directly to the Place appointed. 'Twas easy for her to find the House, the *good Woman* of it waited at the Door for her Approach, and conducted her in: But 'tis hard to say whether her Astonishment or Fear was most predominant, when, instead of *Florez* she found herself accosted by Don *Ferdinand*. Glad would she have been to have had it in her Power to have gone back; and pretending to have come in only through Mistake, would fain have struggled to the Door. *No, lovely Creature,* cry'd the o'er-joy'd *Ferdinand*, (who guessing what her Intent wou'd be, had taken care to hold fast both her Hands,) *to what good Star soever I am indebted for this Blessing, I should prove myself strangely unworthy of it, could I so easily be brought to quit it.—I long have languish'd with a Passion great as your own unequall'd Charms, and for an Opportunity to tell you so, wou'd have hazarded more than my Life.—Hear it then now with Patience, nor Hate the Man who aims at no higher Happiness from your Favour, than to be pitied, and forgiven.* These last Words dissipated great Part of the Terror she had been in; and reassuming that Air of Haughtiness which her Disorders had a little abated, *I know not, my Lord*, answer'd she, *whether I should consider what you have said to me as the Effects of Gaiety, or Sincerity: If to the former, I ought not to resent it, because few Men but would have behav'd in the same manner to a Woman whom Chance had so unexpectedly thrown in their way: But if to the latter, when future Services shall testify it, I owe more to the Quality and Merits of Don* Ferdinand, *than not to acknowledge myself oblig'd to his Regard. You are divinely good,* resum'd the other, *and I hope, since I am but too sensible, whatever Accident occasion'd me this Happiness, it was not Chance, but the Design of meeting a more favour'd Lover brought you here, you will permit me to entertain you with the History of my Passion, at least till his Approach shall cut me off.*

That Serenity which had so lately return'd to the Soul of *Idalia*, at hearing this, again forsook her; she had no room to doubt the Secret of her Correspondence with *Florez* was discover'd: And, in a Moment, had a thousand various Conjectures by what means, but had too great an Opinion of her own Power, and his Passion, to hit upon the right. She was silent for sometime, not knowing whether it was best to confess, or deny the Truth of what he alledg'd; at last, reflecting on the Confidence with which Don *Ferdinand* had spoke, was an Evidence he was assured of it; and that the coming of *Florez*, whom she expected every Moment, would render all she could say ineffectual, concluded on acknowledging the Reality; but withal told him, as she very well might, that it was not to gratify any other Passion than the Love of a little unmeaning Gallantry in her Humour, which had moved her to consent to such a Meeting. This Declaration seem'd to transport the Soul of him 'twas made to; and he continued to address her with so much elegant Tenderness, and lively Assurances of the Influence of her Charms, that the Conversation would have afforded her an Infinity of Satisfaction, had it been at any other Time and Place; but the Disrespect she imagin'd herself treated with by the Delay of *Florez*, poison'd the Felicity which else the gaining a new Adorer of Don *Ferdinand's* Rank would have given her: She sat for a considerable Time divided between Pain and Pleasure, till it growing late, and not knowing what Excuse to make for being so long miss'd at home, she rose to take her leave: But, alas! she was now in a Place whence it was not usual for one of her Sex to return as they came in, and in the Power of one who was not of a Humour to put a Constraint on his Inclinations. She soon perceiv'd the fatal Truth, and now condemn'd the indiscreet Hazard she had run, resolv'd in her Mind never to be guilty of the like, and begg'd of Heaven to protect her Honour, and inspire her with some Artifice with which she might elude the Danger which so imminently threaten'd her.

But what Miseries sometimes does one rash Action bring on the whole Series of Life? Repentance, and a sudden Abhorrence of that Vanity which had led her into this Snare, were now in vain: Her evil Genius watch'd this Point of Time, when every friendly Planet was oppress'd, and only raging Influences govern'd, to ruin her, at *once*, forever. At first, with Sighs, with Tears, with humble Adorations, the amorous *Ferdinand* sought to melt her into Kindness; but they railing, the burning Passion threw off all Restraint, his every Action spoke his Resolution, and told her he would not be denied.—Plainly she read it in his fiery Eyes, and felt it in his eager Graspings.—The Reader's Imagination here can only form an Idea of that Confusion, that mingled Rage and Horror, which, at this dreadful Exigence, fill'd the Soul of the unhappy *Idalia!* 'Tis not in Words to represent it!—Sometimes, disdainful of the injurious Attempt, her stormy Anger vented itself in Curses; but then remembering how little she had the Power of resisting whatever his wild Desires might prompt him to commit, she sunk to milder Treatment, wept, begg'd him to desist:—Prayers,—Threat'nings,— Entreaties, and Revilings, alternately succeeded, as the different Agitations rose in her Breast, till at last she had no Breath to utter either. Her Spirits, fatigued with this unusual Hurry, and all her Limbs tir'd in the Struggle with such unequal Strength, she fainted as he held her in his Arms. As much bent as he was on making himself Master of his Wishes, he could not resolve to indulge them so far as to take any immodest Advantage of this Opportunity; but endeavouring by gentle Means to bring her to herself, and expressing the most tender Concern imaginable for the Disorder he had occasion'd her, she began, at the Return of Thought, to hope his Sentiments were chang'd; and falling on her Knees the Moment she recover'd, *O my* Lord, said she, *if Honour, Love, or Pity, have any Influence over your Soul, by that I wou'd conjure you to forbear to fright a wretched Maid, whom Inadvertency has thrown into your Power. Permit me to depart uninjur'd, unpolluted, and here I swear by everything that's sacred, of all your Sex you shall be dearest to me.—O moving Words*, interrupted *Ferdinand! What Wonders may they not inforce? Is it then possible that you do not hate me?—But*, continued he with a Sigh, *how full of Vanity must I be to credit them?—No, Madam, no, the Artifice is plain; you fear my Power, and would delude my Wishes by a false Hope; but know I love too well, too violently, to leave ought to* hereafter, *which* this Moment *may bestow.—If you would have me think you mean my Happiness, give me an instant Proof:*—Now *make me blest, and I shall feed Imagination with Hope of* future *Favours.*—In speaking this, he mingled some Freedoms, which left but little Room to hope that anything could save her; yet, thinking still to sooth him would be the most effectual Way, *O! Heavens!* resum'd she, *(struggling with all her Force,) will you not then allow something to my Sex's Modesty? Time and Assiduity may make me yours, and spare you the Guilt of Force.*— He would not suffer her to proceed, but renewing his Pressures, *To wait a slow Consent*, said he, *would little suit the Violence of a Passion, such as I profess. The God of Love disdains all dull Delays:—Swiftly the* zealous *Votary rushes on his Wish, and baffles Opposition; cuts off, at once, Sighs, Tears, Entreaties, all the Repulses that stubborn Virtue or Affectation inspire in the relentless Fair, and proves the* Deity indeed, *Almighty.—Believe me, lovely Maid, the whining Wretch who sues at slavish Distance, dies at your Feet, nor dares aspire to seize what Passion aims at, is but in Shew a Lover, the Flame he boasts enervate, weak, and spiritless, like his Attacks; but I by Deeds shall testify how much—How much thou art a Villian*, (cried *Idalia*, transported, at once, with Horror, Shame, and Rage,) *thou Monster! thou brutal Ravisher! But since thou hast lost all Regard due to thy own Honour, and my Birth and Fame, die*, (continued she, snatching a Dagger, which, his upper Garment flying open in the Struggle, just then discover'd itself,) *die by her Hand whom thou so basely dost attempt to wrong*. It was as much as he could do, by leaping lightly from her, toward the Blow her Indignation had design'd. It would have been easy for him to have wrested it from her afterwards; but she perceiving his Intent, turn'd the Point to her own Breast, and invoking all the Saints and Angels to be Witnesses of her Vow, swore she would strike it thro' her Heart the Moment he attempted to disarm her. *No, barbarous Man*, (pursu'd she,) *whatever mistaken Notions the Levity and fond Belief of some of our weak Sex may have inspired thee with, thou now shalt find there's one among us who dares meet Death to fly Dishonour.—Since deaf to all the Considerations of my noble Family, and* Bernardo's *Power, behold and tremble at my* Virtue's *Bravery:—Blest now with Means to escape thy vile Design, I can no longer fear thee, nor need debase my just Disdain so far as to entreat thee.* The Fire which now darted from her Eyes, the assured Accent of her Voice, and the resolute Air of all her Motions, sufficiently declared she would make no scruple of fulfilling the Protestation she had made. Don *Ferdinand* was too sensibly alarm'd at it, to put it to the Venture, but immediately form'd a Stratagem which seem'd more likely to succeed: Making use, therefore, of that Dissimulation which those who study the undoing Art are so well vers'd in, he dress'd his Eyes and Face in Looks far different from those they lately wore; an humble Admiration now seem'd to take up all his Thoughts, and aw'd Desire seem'd fearful to appear: He prostrated himself before her, acknowledged the Temerity of his Attempt, conjured her either to forgive him, or plunge the Dagger where she first design'd it, swore he would not live in her Displeasure; and accompanied all he said with so many Sighs, and such well-counterfeited Contrition, that either her Vanity, (which often inclines Women too readily to pardon those Faults which they imagine caused by the Force of their own Charms, and the Violence of the Lover's Passion,) her good Nature, or perhaps a secret Liking of his Person, made it impossible for her to deny what he so earnestly entreated. The Grant, however, was not without Limitation; she forgave all he had done, but on Condition he should never repeat it, and that he would not oppose her immediate Return to her Father's House. *Far be it from my Thoughts*, replied the artful *Ferdinand; this Moment would I deny my fond gazing Eyes the Joy of looking on you, had I not yet one Request to make, which, if refused, I have no more to do but die. What is it?* said *Idalia. After having obtain'd a Pardon for your injurious Design upon my Honour, it must be something beyond what I can comprehend that I should think difficult to grant. Love ever is accompanied with Fears*, resum'd he; *and that it is something relating to that, the Terrors I am in to ask it, may inform you. Let me conjure you, then, by all that heavenly Softness in your Disposition, to tell me, and tell me truly, (for fain would I flatter my ambitious Wishes with a Hope my Services, in time, might move you,) if I can gain your noble* Father's *Leave to make my humble Application, will you consent to hear me? Is not there something in my Form or Manner, which will repel the soft Efforts of Love?—O speak!* (continued he, perceiving she was silent,) *I dread the* Certainty, *yet am unable to endure the Tortures of* Suspense.—*I know not*, answer'd she, blushing, *if it be consistent with a Virgin's Modesty, to answer a Demand like this, but something sure must be allow'd to the Quality and Merits of Don* Ferdinand; *nor will my Sex condemn my easy Nature, when to such exalted Accomplishments I throw off Affectation, and confess I shall, with Pride and Pleasure, listen to the Vows my* Father *shall command me to receive from you.*

ELIZA HAYWOOD

Tho' nothing could be more distant from the Soul of Don *Ferdinand* than the Design of solliciting *Bernardo* on any such Account, yet the feigning it was of infinite Service to gain Time, which was all he wanted. Examining the Hours, they found the Night was so far spent, that *Idalia* was at her Wit's End to think what Excuse she should make for her long Absence. *Ferdinand* taking the Advantage of her Fear, *Madam*, said he, *tho' I much doubt all I can say, after the Presumption I have been guilty of, will be suspected, I would advise you not to go home till Morning: You will have Time enough by then to think of something plausible to allay your Father's Concern;—or you may go early to some Lady of your Acquaintance, and engage her to pretend you have been with her all Night.—Till then, this House is at your Devotion; you shall be serv'd in all your command; and, to prevent your Fears of my relapsing into my late Error, I will myself go out of it.* What cannot an artful Dissimulation engage one to? *Idalia* believed him now so entirely her Convert, that what he counsell'd did not in the least alarm her; and the good Opinion she now had of him, and the Uncertainty in what Manner she could excuse herself at home, made her willing to accept it. She had a little Shock, however, at lying at a House, which, by the Liberties Don *Ferdinand* had taken in it, she could not imagine to be held by People of Honour; but the seeming penitent Lover removing that Scruple by assuring her that they were so much at his Devotion, that as soon as they saw there was an Alteration in his Humour, theirs would immediately acquiesce, she at last consented to remain there till Morning; but told him, she expected the Performance of his Promise of going away himself. *Madam*, (answered he,) *not all the Reluctance I feel in myself at quitting the Roof where all my Hopes are treasur'd, shall oblige me to disobey you. I go this Moment; and that no needless Fears may disturb the Repose I wish you, I entreat you will see me from the Door, and take with you the Key, which alone could be the Passport to admit me here again.* *Idalia* was so well pleas'd with the Care he express'd of her Quiet, that she again, at his Entreaty, confirm'd the Pardon she had already granted, and took leave of him, with a Countenance which testified her Words were in no way contradictory to her Heart.

After his Departure, having taken the Key, as he desired her to do, into her Possession, she suffer'd herself to be conducted by the People of the House into a Chamber, and was not long before she went to Bed: But it was impossible for Sleep to have any Power over her; Imagination was too busy to suffer the dull God's Approach; the Pleasure she took in being admir'd was too much rooted in her Nature, for the late Danger it had brought her into, to eraze; and the Joy of having an Adorer, such as Don *Ferdinand*, made full Amends for the Frights some Part of his Behaviour had put her in. From this Contemplation, which afforded her only *Delights*, she fell into one altogether as *vexatious*, which was the Neglect that *Florez* had treated her with, in not coming to the Place he had appointed her to be at; and if she could have believed it possible for any Man, who had seen her, to *resign* her to a Rival, she would not have been a Stranger to the Truth; for she, as well as all who had Acquaintance with him, was sensible to the Obligations he had to *Ferdinand*. But this was the last Reason she could form; it was not without the greatest Difficulty in the World she could bring herself to any Notion of it, and perhaps she should have found out someother Motive for his Behaviour, less disagreeable to her to believe, if her Cogitations had not met with an Interruption she was far from thinking of.

She had look'd on herself as safe where she now was, as in her *Father's* House, thro' the double Security of her *Lover's* Conversion, and having the Key of the Door: But, alas! she too soon discover'd her Mistake. She had not been an Hour in Bed, before she felt the Clothes thrown off, and something catch fast hold of her. The Voice and Actions of the Person told her it was no other than Don *Ferdinand*, as did his own Behaviour and Confession afterward, that the Story of his Repentance was but forg'd, the easier to betray her, and the Delivery of the Key only an Artifice to engage her Trust, there being a Back-Door to the House, by which he immediately enter'd, and came into the Chamber thro' a Closet, which had a Passage into another Room.

What was now the Distraction of this unhappy Lady, waked from her Dream of Vanity to certain Ruin! unavoidable Destruction! She rav'd, she tore, did all that Women could; but all in vain!—In the midst of Shrieks and Tremblings, Cries, Curses, Swoonings, the impatient *Ferdinand* perpetrated his Intent, and finish'd her Undoing.

In the mean time, the careful *Father* had been in all the Anxiety imaginable: He had sent to every Place where he had Hope to find her, in search of his darling Daughter; till at last, all his Endeavours being vain, and the Lateness of the Night not bringing her, assured him she could not be detained by any Occasion which could merit his Approbation, he flew into her Chamber, broke open her Cabinet, believing there might be a Probability of some Discovery; and finding there the Letters

ELIZA HAYWOOD

she had received from *Florez*, and, amongst the rest, that last fatal one which mention'd the Place of Assignation, he concluded her lost; that either she had disposed of herself to some unworthy Match, or had been deluded into a much worse Inconvenience. He could do nothing till Morning, either for his Satisfaction of Revenge; and all who have known the Grief of a beloved Child's Undoing, will easy guess at his. At Break of Day he sent to the Officers of Justice for a *Mission* to search that House, and produced the Paper which had occasion'd his requiring it. It was immediately granted; and he had soon been inform'd of the whole Transaction, had not the strangest Accident that ever was, skreened the injurious Contrivers of it for sometime from the Punishments their Crime was worthy of.

Don *Ferdinand* was endeavouring, by all the Perswasions he was Master of, to bring the ruin'd Fair to an Opinion she was not so unhappy as she thought herself; but all that he could say was ineffectual to give a Moment's Cessation to the Tempest of her Fury: Had any Means of Death been in her Power, she would certainly not have out-lived the Loss of Honour; but as he had taken care of that, all she cou'd do, was to lament it. As they were thus employed, a loud Knocking at the Chamber-Door obliged the surpris'd Lover to quit his Bed, and see what had occasion'd it. It was *Florez*, who happening to pass by Don *Bernardo's* Door, had seen a great Crowd about it; and enquiring the Reason, was told, They were going in search of the young Lady of that House, who, 'twas thought, had been convey'd away by a Gentleman who pretended to court her.—This News was sufficient to alarm the guilty Soul of him 'twas told to; and not doubting but everything was discovered, had hasted to *Ferdinand* to apprize him of it.—*Without doubt*, said he, *my Lord, the whole Secret is betray'd, and I, and the People of this House must be inevitably ruin'd, as Abettors of the Fact, unless your Interest with the* Doge *is strong enough to protect us. My Interest with my Uncle*, replied the other, very much perplexed, *I fear will be too weak even to obtain a Pardon for myself in an Affair like this:*—Bernardo *is a Senator, and highly esteemed both by the Court and the Populace:—I know not what to think on it.*—He stood a for a Moment or two after he had spoke this in a Pause; and that gave *Idalia* (who, by the Coming of *Florez*, and the Advertisement he brought, knew it was to his Deceit she ow'd her Ruin) Liberty to vent some Part of her just Rage in Curses and Reproaches. Neither of them in that Confusion seem'd to take much Notice of what she said; but Don *Ferdinand* starting from his

Musing, and catching up his Clothes, and putting them on as fast as he could, *'Tis now no Time*, said he, *to answer idle Railing, we must prepare for our common Safety.* As soon as he had spoke these Words, he call'd for the Woman of the House, who presently came up, frighted almost to Death with the Account she had receiv'd from *Florez*, and order'd her to dress *Idalia* with all the Expedition imaginable, bidding her not to be concern'd, for he had bethought him of a Way to retrieve all. But all that he, or she, or *Florez* could do, was not to any purpose to perswade *Idalia* to rise: She seem'd, in the midst of her Anguish, to exult with Hope of Vengeance, and swore she would continue in the very Place and Posture she was in; and, by proclaiming her Wrongs, and the Authors of them, put it past the Power of all their Artifice to escape the Punishment they feared. But, alas! her Resolution stood her but in little stead on this Occasion, the imminent Danger they were in made them dispense with Ceremony, and she was taken out of Bed by Force, and her Clothes, in what Manner they could, huddled on. As soon as she was made (made) ready, he catch'd her in his Arms, and carried her down Stairs, bidding *Florez* look that nothing was left in the Chamber which might discover who had been there. The House that join'd to that in which they were, belong'd to a young Gentleman whose Name was *Henriquez de Valago*, an intimate Friend and Companion of *Ferdinand's*: Thither did he carry the disconsolate *Idalia*, entreating him to be careful that her Despair acted nothing against her Life; and that he would conceal her from the View of all his Servants, and at Night convey her to *Padua*, to a Seat he knew he had in that City. *Henriquez* having faithfully promised to obey him in all these Injunctions, he left him, and return'd to *Florez* and the *Landlady*: The latter he bad be of good Comfort, there could be no Proof against her; and all she had to do, was to be resolute in her Denials; for which, he told her, he would not fail to recompence her. Having given this necessary Order, he went away with *Florez* at the Back-Door the very Moment that *Bernardo*, and those he brought, were commanding the other to be opened. The Woman, according to Directions, immediately obey'd, and so well counterfeited a Surprise at the Demands they made, that a Person less interested than Don *Bernardo* would have believ'd her innocent; but the Letter was to him an Evidence substantial; and tho' in searching all the Rooms, examining the Servants, and taking all the Care usual on such Occasions, there seem'd not the least Ground to imagine she, or any other Persons, beside the Family, had been there, he was obliged to go away more *unsatisfy'd*, because he wanted Proof, but as much *assured* as before, that this was the fatal Place which had deprived him of his Daughter.

*Ferdinand,* accompany'd by *Florez*, went directly to his own Apartment; where having passed sometime in Consultation in what Manner it was best to proceed, at last it was concluded, that the latter should remain there conceal'd, till they should find out by what Means the Discovery had been made; and it being the Custom of the former every Morning to attend the *Doge*, he now dressed him, and at the usual Hour went to the Palace, which he found crowded by a great Number of the Nobility and Senators, who, he was inform'd by some of them, were summon'd by the *Doge* on an Affair relating to Don *Bernardo*. It is easy to believe his Thoughts were not a little perplex'd, to find the Affair had made so great a Noise; but veiling his Confusion as much as possible, he mingled with the Company that were going into the Room where his Uncle expected to receive them. The Morning Salutations were scarce over, when the unhappy *Bernardo* enter'd, and made his Complaint with so moving an Air, that few that heard him, but pity'd his Misfortune. The *Doge* entreated him to be of Comfort, assured him, that nothing in the Compass of his Power should be wanting for his Redress; and that, if by any Means the Person who had injur'd him could be detected, the Offender, tho' found in the nearest and most dear Relation of his own, should not be protected from the severest Punishment the Law or his Revenge requir'd. The mournful Father made his Compliment for these Assurances in as handsome a Manner as his Grief would give him leave; and having finish'd it, proceeded to relate all the Circumstances he knew of his Misfortune, which was the finding of the Letters, one of which had so punctually nominated *that House* for the Place she was to come to; but that having been search'd, and nothing of Proof to be made that she had been there, it was not impossible but some Person, to confound their Examination, might have writ it on Purpose. All that remain'd was to endeavour to discover by whom these Letters were writ, for there was no Name to any of them, (*Idalia* having forbid it, that her Correspondence with *Florez* might not by any Accident be fount out.) *Bernardo* produced them to the View of the whole Assembly, and the *Doge* earnestly adjur'd all present, that if they could in the least guess by the Style or Character who was the Author, they would immediately declare it: But everyone affirm'd himself entirely ignorant; and *Ferdinand* now hugg'd himself in a full Security that this first Brunt being past, nothing could hereafter prejudice him, or *Florez*, on the Account of *Idalia*: But the Solemnity with which he had heard his Uncle protest to Don *Bernardo*, that if the Person who had wrong'd him could by any Means be discover'd, the strictest Severity of Justice should be his Portion, made him extremely cautious in what Manner he behav'd. He forbore, therefore, to visit *Idalia* while she was conceal'd at the House of Don *Henriquez*, nor would for some Days after he knew she was carry'd to *Padua*, go there.

But while the Success of this Adventure afforded a good deal of satisfactory Matter of Conversation to those who were the Contrivers of it, whenever they were together, the miserable *Bernardo* pass'd his Hours in a Condition pityable by all but those who had occasion'd it: He refused to eat or drink, shut himself from all Society, and suffer'd not the Light of Heaven to enter at his mournful Windows. In vain his Friends, Relations, and Acquaintance, endeavour'd to perswade him to asswage his Sorrows;—in vain the *Religious* of all Orders sent their daily Remonstrances, how unlawful it was to give Way to such immoderate Grief! He was not to be mov'd;—he was not to be comforted;—and it was look'd on as almost a Miracle, that *Age*, so oppress'd, sunk not beneath the Burden of an Anguish sufficient to have weigh'd down *Youth*.

But to return to *Idalia*:—Never Man had a Task more difficult, than *Henriquez* found in executing the Charge Don *Ferdinand* had given him. That wretched Lady was so bent on Death, that there requir'd the utmost Caution to prevent the Mischief which her Fury threaten'd; a hundred Times, in that one Day she remain'd in his House, had she attempted on her Life; and when he had put her into a *Gondula*, which he had order'd to be made ready for that purpose, he was obliged to hold her the whole Time of their little Voyage in his Arms, or the River *Brent* had been her Grave. *O cruel, barbarous Man!* said she, *why will you deny me the only Relief for Miseries like mine?—But think not to disappoint me always:—Not all the Powers of Heaven and Earth combined shall force me long to drag this Load of Infamy and Woe! I cannot,—will not live!*—With such like Speeches, which were still accompany'd with tearing of her Hair, her Garments, and sometimes her very Flesh, did she express the bitter Anguish of her Soul, whenever he attempted to divert her Desperation: But how dangerous is it for a Heart young and amorous to entertain Compassion for a lovely Object! what a prevailing Force has Beauty in Distress! not all her Distraction, nor the wild Horror which sat on her Features, could take from them their Power

ELIZA HAYWOOD

of Charming.—The Fire of Indignation which sparkled in her Eyes abated not the wonted Sweetness,—the very Confusion of her Air had something graceful in it; and *Henriquez* too soon was sensible, that in the Design of serving *Ferdinand* he had undertaken an Office fatal to his own Repose. He struggled, however, with all the Force he was able, to withstand the first Emotions of his Passion, not only because of the Injustice such Sentiments would make him guilty of to a Friend who had entrusted him, but also that himself was under Obligations of Constancy to a Lady who had preferr'd him to the whole World.

But, alas! what Ties, what Obligations, what Engagements are sufficient to bind the roving Heart of faithless Man? Untasted Pleasures still are thought the sweetest!: *Donna Lawra* (for so was she call'd, the Memory of whose Charms this new Beauty was beginning to eraze) had already been too bounteous of her Favours to make the almost fated *Henriquez* over sollicitous of the Continuance of them: He had, however, more Gratitude than many of his Sex can boast, and, as I have already said, endeavour'd for sometime very strenuously to repel the Assaults of any new Desires to her Prejudice; and 'tis not altogether *impossible* (though not exceeding *probable*, considering the Charms of *Idalia*, and the Inconstancy which is natural to Mankind) that his Efforts might not have been unsuccessful, had not herself contributed to her Undoing.

Never Woman was of a more haughty, jealous, and impatient Disposition, than this Lady; and having sometime before made *Henriquez* a Present of a little *Moorish* Page, with a Design to be a Spy on his Actions, was by him inform'd that his Master had order'd a *Gondula* to wait him about Sun-set at the River *Brent*; and that he had commanded his Servants not to discover to any Person after his Departure which Way he was gone. This was sufficient to alarm her with an Apprehension, that something must have occasion'd this Secrecy; and the rather, because she had sent twice that Day to desire to speak with him, and he had both Times excused himself from coming, pretending Indisposition. She immediately, as jealous Women do, imagin'd the worst, was certain in her own Mind that a new Mistress had engaged him from her, and that it could be with no other he intended to leave *Venice*: She presently suppos'd it must be to *Padua* he was going; and not able to linger in the Torments of Suspence, resolv'd to be there before him; and that no Notice might be taken of her Design, would not command her own *Gondula*, tho' she had a very fine one, to be prepared, but got into one of those common *Wherries* which generally wait to carry ordinary Passengers. She had frequently been at the House which Don *Henriquez* had at *Padua*, and the Servants that were in it perfectly knew her, and were not at all surpris'd to see her, especially when she told them that their Master would be there next Morning. But the Confusion with which *Henriquez* at his Arrival beheld her there, may more easily be imagin'd than described; therefore I shall only say it was such as could be surmounted by nothing but the Indignation of *Lawra*, when, by the Sight of *Idalia* with him, she had so much Reason to believe her Suspicions were too just: She flew on him with all the Reproaches that her Rage, and the Confirmation of her Jealously, could suggest; to which he gave but little Answer, till after he had conducted his lovely *Charge* to a Chamber, and appointed a Servant to watch and attend her. At his Return to the Room where he had left *Lawra*, he endeavour'd to allay the Fury she was in, by telling her part of the Truth: He assured her that it was not on his own Account that he had been at the Pains of bringing that Lady thither, but conceal'd the Name of the Person for whose sake he had done it, being of that Opinion which most of his Sex have of the other, that there was but little Security for their Secrecy, and was sensible how dangerous for *Ferdinand* it would be, if by her Levity it should be revealed. But his evading to let her into the whole Affair, render'd her incapable of believing any Part of it; all that he could say seem'd but so many Excuses, and was ineffectual to alleviate her Passion.—She loaded him with Curses and Upbraidings,—swore never to see him more.—Nor could all his Entreaties prevail on her to continue a Moment longer in his House; but taking Advantage of the *Gondula* which had brought him and *Idalia*, left him, with a Vow never to rest till she had meditated a Revenge suitable to his Perfidiousness.

When once a Woman has disposed of everything in her Power to give, it must be Softness only, and fond Compliance with her Lover's Will, that can maintain her Empire o'er his Heart.—The Power which once this Lady had, was already shock'd by the newer and more potent Charms of the incomparable *Idalia*; and the Violence of her impatient Jealously bringing to his Remembrance a thousand Faults in her Humour, which in the *Noon* of a Passion's Sun were hid, but now, in the *Wane* of his Affections, appear'd in their worst Colours, she began not only to appear distasteful to his softer Sentiments, but also to seem justly so to those which Reason had the greatest Share in inspiring.—He knew not, however, to what Extremes her Indignation might transport her; and to prevent what she might contrive, thought it the best way to remove *Idalia*. He had a little *Villa* at *Vicenza*, about a Day's Journey from *Padua*, in the Road to *Verona*, one of the most pleasantly situated *Places* in all *Italy*, having its Foundation on a Hill, which afforded a Prospect of the whole Country round for many Miles. The Sweetness of the Air, and the Variety of rural Diversions she might find there, he hop'd might have an Influence over her Melancholy, and in time wear off the Bitterness of those agonizing Reflections which at present she was so full of.

He delayed the Execution of this Design no longer than the next Day; and as nothing violent is ever of any long Continuance, thro' his Perswasions, and the Measures he made use of to effect it, the desperate Emotions which had raged with so much Fury in the Soul of *Idalia*, began by little and little to abate; and the wonderful Respect, and prodigious Tenderness with which she found herself treated by this new Adorer, by degrees entirely reconciled her to Life. He observ'd it with Joy; and being desirous to discover more, one Day, as they were sitting together, he entreated her to command him something whereby he might testify the sincere Esteem and Admiration he professed to have for her.—He assured her there was nothing so difficult that he would not undertake for her sake; and to sound her Inclinations, begg'd she wou'd have Confidence enough in him to acquaint him with what she would have done:—*Do not, Madam*, said he, *consider yourself as under any Restraint, while at* Vicenza: *Tho' nothing in the World can afford me a Joy adequate to that of gazing on you, yet if you are determined to return to your Father, myself shall conduct you to him, and endeavour to invent some Excuse which may shadow over the true Cause of your Absence:—Or if you can enough to forgive the Faults of raging Passion, to yield to the Affections of Don* Ferdinand, *tho' to the eternal Ruin of my own ardent Wishes, at* Padua, *you shall meet him; for doubtless he will soon be there to take you from me:— Or if there be anything in this Place so agreeable to you, as to make you willing to bless me with you Residence in it, here remain safe both from your Father's Power, and the Sollicitations of all you would avoid.* This Officer appeared so generous, that *Idalia* was infinitely charm'd with it; and after a little Pause, *I am so much oblig'd*, reply'd she, *to your Honour and good Nature, since I have been here, that it is not without the utmost Confusion I reflect on my Manner of treating you when I was first put in your Power. As you had no hand in my Undoing, I ought to have reserved my Reproaches for those who alone are worthy of them;—and to the rest of your Obligations I see you are willing to add that of pardoning what my Madness uttered: But*, continued she, with an Air wholly composed of Sweetness, *for this last Favour I know not with what Words to thank you:—There's something in it beyond the Reach of Gratitude;—and 'tis in my Acceptance only that I can prove how truly I am touch'd with it.—To return to* Venice *I never can consent: My Reputation blasted, and ruin'd by my Father's hasty Zeal, in publishing this Adventure, I shou'd become the Jest of every sawcy Girl that envy'd me before:—My Spirit cou'd not bear it.—No, first I'd turn a wretched Wanderer thro' the pitiless World!—a Grave wou'd now be preferable to my Father's House!—But as to* Ferdinand!—*the Villain!—the Monster that has undone me!—Hell, Hell, is not so dreadful as the Thoughts of seeing him again!—Then, Madam*, cry'd the transported *Henriquez*, interrupting her, *I may hope you will continue here? For sometime*, resum'd she; *if you grow not weary of so troublesome a Guest, I'll stay till I have disposed of myself either in a Monastery, or someother Place.* 'Tis easy to suppose with how much Rapture the enamour'd *Henriquez* heard her speak these Words: There passed between 'em several Protestations of Love and Adoration on the one side, and Esteem and Gratitude on the other; and at last entring into a Discourse what Method was most proper to make use of for the preserving her in that Liberty she desir'd, they both thought it best that he should leave her there, and return to *Padua* before the coming of *Ferdinand*; and missing him, should discover he had carry'd her to any other Place; and that at their first meeting, he should counterfeit the greatest Concern imaginable for not having been able to discharge the Trust reposed in him; and withal, dress up a Story of her having made her escape by Night from his House. This being concluded on, he took Horse immediately for *Padua*, where had happened a Disturbance he little expected to hear of.

The malicious *Lawra*, doubly disappointed in her Love and Pride, meditated nothing but Revenge; and tho' she had never seen *Idalia* before she met her at *Henriquez's* House, nor could be certain she was that Lady whose Elopement had made so great a Noise at *Venice*, yet it came into her Head to report it, not doubting but Don *Bernardo* would take such measures to assure himself, as would infallibly expose her Rival. She thought, that if it were really *Idalia*, as there was nothing improbable but it should, the Father's just Indignation would not only be the Ruin of his Passion, by depriving him of her Sight forever, but also the eternal Destruction of his Fortune, and perhaps his Life; for there was not anything too violent for her Rage to wish inflicted on him: And that if it should happen to be any other Woman, the Discovery who she was, and the Opportunity it would give of blasting her Reputation, would be some little Satisfaction for the Loss of *Henriquez*. With this View she took a Pen, and employ'd it to Don *Bernardo*, in the Manner following:

## To Don BERNARDO

To receive an Injury, yet to be, by our Ignorance of the Person who offers it, deprived of the Means either of Vengeance or Redress, I look upon as a Vexation almost equal to what the Misfortune itself occasions; and have too great a Sense of what a Father's Heart must feel in a Disappointment like yours, to withold a Secret which may afford some sort of a Satisfaction to you.

The fair *Idalia*, your unhappy Daughter, either too fatally ensnared by the Insinuations of the most Vicious and Perfidious of his Sex Don *Henriquez de Velago*, or betray'd to his Power by some Artifice yet more base, was lodg'd in his House, perhaps in his Bed, when you were vainly searching for her in another Place: But he, with reason, fearing the amorous Theft unsafe to be long detain'd at *Venice*, has since carry'd her to *Padua*, where he now revels in her Ruin, and triumphs in Security.

'Twould be but impertinent to instruct you what to do; you own Wisdom and Parental Care will need no Admonitions with what Expedition you shou'd haste, I will not say to *save*, but to *revenge* a Daughter; therefore will trouble you no farther than to entreat your Pardon for not setting any Name to this Advertisement, which is design'd a friendly one, from

Your unknown Humble Servant

A

A Reader of the most ordinary Capacity will easily imagine this Letter had the Effect on Don *Bernardo* it was writ for: He forgot his Age, and the Indisposition his late Griefs had thrown him in; he deferr'd going to *Padua* no longer a Time than the Necessity of getting those People who were to accompany him requir'd: But this unhappy Gentleman had to his other Calamity this added, of being twice as he believ'd at the Point of detecting the Author of his Misfortune, and as often finding his Expectations disappointed; for the Servants of *Henriquez* were all of them too faithful to utter the least Syllable of what they knew; and *Bernardo* doubted not but he had been a second Time abused, and presently imagin'd the Person who had writ the other Letter to amuse his Search, had also been the Contriver of this.

But tho' there was nothing of *Idalia* to be heard, this Adventure was the Occasion of bringing to light another Secret; which afterward being blaz'd abroad, was Matter enough of Discourse for the whole Town for a long time. Having left *Henriquez's* House, with a Design never to trouble any other without some more evident Demonstration that they were not imposed on, as they pass'd by a Vineyard adjoining to it, they happen'd to see a Country Fellow pruning the Vines; it came into the Head of someone of those who were with *Bernardo*, to enquire of him if he had not seen a Lady at his Master's. The Rustick's Simplicity gave hopes he would not deny the Truth, or if he did, it would be in such a manner, as they might easily discover it; and indeed had a Secret been in his keeping, there was little Probability it would long continue so. He presently told them, a Lady had been there some few Days before; and, said he, 'tis rumour'd here at *Padua*, that she is Don *Henriquez's* Mistress.—Some say that he is to marry her, but by the Mass I believe nothing of it; for chancing to be in the *Grove* behind the House, who did I see come in but these two kissing and toying; they did not think I took any Notice.—I say no more; but if ever he is her Husband, I have lost my Aim—that's all.—These Words, which could not be imagin'd to be utter'd with any other Design than what the Manner of them express'd, the Pleasure some People, especially of his Degree, take in speaking all they know, made poor *Bernardo* ready to sink into the Earth: He was now sure it was *Idalia* that the Fellow meant, and the Horror which seiz'd his before half-broken Heart, was now so great, to hear this seeming Confirmation of the Dishonour of his Family and Ruin of his Child, that he had neither Voice or Spirit to ask more. But the others, being less interested in what they heard, had Presence of Mind enough to put many other Questions to him; among the rest, what sort of a Woman she was who had been so familiar with Don *Henriquez*; if she was tall or short, black or fair; of what Age she appeared to be; and if he had ever seen her before, or knew of her having been at his Master's House any other Time than that he spoke of in the *Grotto*. To most of these Interrogatories the Fellow made such Replies as gave no Certainty whether it was the Lady they were in search of, or not; till to the last, that of how often she had been there, he told them, it had been her constant Custom to come and tarry two or three Nights at a Time, whenever *Henriquez* was at *Padua*, as long as he had been employ'd in working there, which had been above two Years. This Account did no way agree with a Belief that it could be *Idalia*, who had never been one Night absent from her Father's House till that fatal one, in which he had begun his Search; which some of 'em saying, and chancing to mention her Name,—*Alas!* cry'd the Countryman, *you are mistaken, Gentlemen, I do not know anything of the Woman you speak of: She I mean is called Donna* Lawra de Savila, *Widow of Don* Jaquez de Savila: *I was once a Servant of her Husband's, and am as well acquainted with her Face as my own.* There was not a Person in this Company but knew this Lady; but there was one among 'em whom these Words did more particularly influence: He had for a long Time had a Passion for her, and finding all the Endeavours he could make use of were in vain to engage any other Return than Disdain, his slighted Tenderness (as 'tis common enough, especially among the *Italians*) was now converted to as violent an Aversion; and nothing on Earth could have been so agreeable to the Sentiments with which he now consider'd her as this Account, which gave him so fair an Opportunity of affronting, and exposing her; which at their Return to *Venice* he took care to do, with such a witty Inveteracy, that the once haughty, gay, admired *Lawra* saw herself in a little time the Ridicule of all who knew her; and not able to endure the Disrespect of those Reflections which even her very Pretence did not silence, and as little in a Capacity of revenging it, her Charms being almost past the Bloom, and her Wealth, by former Extravagencies very near exhausted, out of Humour with the World, and detesting all Mankind, she retir'd to a Relation's House which few resorted to, who had any Knowledge of her, and indulg'd her Discontent, that a Misfortune she design'd another, had so justly fallen on herself.

But this happen'd not till after she had seen one Part of her indignant Wish fulfill'd, the Death of *Henriquez*; which, tho' not brought about by any Contrivance of her own, she look'd upon as inflicted on him by the Justice of Providence, for his Ingratitude and Perfidiousness to her.

At his Return to *Padua*, 'tis hard to say whether his Surprise to hear his House had been search'd, or the Joy he conceiv'd that the Danger of it was so well over, had the greatest Share in his Soul. But his Contentment was only of a short Continuance: Designing to go immediately to *Venice*, thinking it the more effectual Way to take off all Apprehensions of Don *Ferdinand's* ever expecting to find *Idalia* with him, to go to him with the Story he had form'd of her Escape, than to wait his coming to seek her at *Padua*. He was just preparing to set out, when he was told that Don *Ferdinand* was alighted at the Gate: He went to receive him with the Familiarity which the long Friendship that had been between them render'd the most obliging; but before he had time to mention what he intended about *Idalia*, the other was beginning to make him a thousand Acknowledgments for the Care he had taken in preserving her for him. *To what an infinite Degree, dear Friend*, said he, *am I oblig'd to you for the Trouble you have had in securing for me a Happiness I must but for your Goodness have been utterly depriv'd of! All that I can say, will be too little to express the Gratitude I feel;—but be assured the Favour shall never die in my Remembrance; each Moment that blesses me with my lov'd* Idalia's *Sight, will also remind me it is to you I am indebted for the Rapture.—Alas, my Lord*, (interrupted *Henriquez*, a little confounded at receiving Thanks for that which he was conscious to himself he was far from deserving.) *I wish to Heaven it had been in my Power to have anyway contributed to your Satisfaction; but all my Endeavours were in vain—I know what you would say*, (cry'd *Ferdinand*, not suffering him to proceed,) *I know the inexorable Fair has been deaf to all the Arguments you could urge in favour of my Passions; but no matter, Time and Assiduity may work upon her, and my continued Tenderness engage her* yielding *to that Joy the Violence of my burning Passion has yet but by* Force *obtain'd.—But haste*, pursu'd he, *my dear* Henriquez! *haste, and conduct me to her;—my throbbing Heart beats high with raging Love;—this tedious Absence which the Fear of being suspected, and by that means losing her forever, could only have occasion'd, has made me almost wild with fierce Impatience!—I burn, I bleed, I die to see her!—Can it be possible*, resum'd *Henriquez* coldly, *this mighty Longing, this ardent Wishing for one whose Charms already you have rifled; can the Desire of Beauty enjoy'd and known, afford such eager Transports?—'Tis strange indeed, reply'd* Ferdinand; *but would not seem so, could you have any Notion how much beyond her Sex* Idalia *is!—how charming, even in the midst of Rage and Grief!—Her very Frowns have more Attractions in 'em than the most melting Softness of any other Woman! I am sorry for it, said* Henriquez *and if Wishes could avail, would willingly lose Part of my Blood, she seem'd less worthy your Esteem.*

The Surprise of the enamour'd *Ferdinand* at these Words can hardly be represented, much less the Rage with which he listen'd to that Story the other had prepar'd to deceive him into a Belief of her Flight. There is nothing in the World more difficult than to conceal *Love* from him who is a *Lover*, but much more so, when the same Object enflames them both; besides, there are so many little Hesitations in the telling an Untruth, especially with those who do not usually practice it, that a nice Observer may easily discern the Difference. Don *Ferdinand* was too passionate an Admirer of *Idalia's* Perfections, not to believe it highly probable another might think of her as he did; and, by the Force he had made use of to gratify his Desires, one might know he was not so great a Bigot to the Rules of Honour, as to imagine they had Power to restrain Appetite. He forbore, however, to interrupt the other while he was speaking; but as he found him silent, he broke out into all the Exclamations the Falshood he believed himself treated with deserved. *Henriquez*, willing to preserve his Friendship, but resolute not to forego *Idalia*, made a thousand Imprecations to aver the Truth of what he said, but to no Purpose; and had it really happen'd as *Henriquez* pretended, 'tis probable he would have found it a hard Matter to have gain'd Credit from this Impatient Lover. Fierce and tempestuous in his Nature when anything displeased him, he let him know he saw through, and disdain'd the feeble Arts with which he went about to impose on him, and bid him once for all bring forth *Idalia*, or answer his Demand with his Sword. *Henriquez* would very fain have evaded either, but finding himself press'd past refusal, and absolutely bent not to comply with the *former*, he was obliged to do so to the *latter*, or prove himself a Coward; the Place agreed on for the Decision of this fatal Controversy, was a Field adjoining to *Henriquez's* House; and *Ferdinand* going there before, to avoid Suspicion of their Quarrel, the other promised to follow him immediately.

It was not without the greatest Concern that *Henriquez* found himself involv'd in this unhappy Necessity, either to be miserable forever in the Loss of *Idalia*, or become the Enemy of a Person whom he had long consider'd as the most intimate of his Friends, and one in whose power it was to do him many ill Offices with the *Doge*; on whom he, as well as the other, had a Dependance. But what Considerations are of force against Love? After two or three moments Reflection, he sat him down, and writ a Letter, which he gave to a trusty Servant, ordering him to carry it with all Secrecy and Speed to his *Villa* at *Vincenza*, and deliver it to *Idalia*; and then immediately went to the Field, where the enraged *Ferdinand* impatiently expected him.

A few words, much to the same purpose as those they had entertain'd each other with in the House, having past between them, the new-made Enemies drew their Swords, and running against each other with greater *Force* than *Art*, each more aiming to reach his Rival's Life than defend his own, both had their Wish; the unfortunate *Henriquez* lost his at the first Push, and his Antagonist having receiv'd his Death's Wound, though yet ignorant of it, seeing him fall, was about to make his Escape, when, on a sudden, he found himself unable, and that he should soon lose both the Triumph of having overcome his Foe, and the Danger of the Punishment the Law inflicts on Duelists. He surviv'd not the other above half an hour, as the Chirurgeons, who afterwards examin'd the Bodies, imagin'd; and the untimely Death of these two unhappy Gentlemen gave *Idalia* the first Proof, that her Beauty, like a fatal Comet, was destructive to all on whom it had any Influence, and seem'd given her in so extraordinary a Proportion, only to make her Misfortunes more conspicuous.

She, who little dreamt of this fatal Catastrophe, was in the mean time, entertaining herself with *Ideas* of a far different nature; had she been less conscious of her own Excellencies, she would not have been blind to the Admiration which every Word and Action testify'd Don *Henriquez* had of them. She saw plainly that he lov'd her, and lov'd her with a Passion which was not to be accounted less violent, because it was more respectful than that of Don *Ferdinand*; her Pride however would certainly have prefer'd the latter, because of his superior Quality, could she have entertain'd the least hope, that after what had happened he would marry her. But young and vain as she was, she flatter'd not herself with such a hope; and for that reason, as well as for the Violence he had used her with he was the Object of her extremest Detestation; but as for *Henriquez*, she began to consider, that if his Designs were honourable, as he had never given her any Cause to suspect they were not, she might, by becoming his Wife, take off all the Odium, which, by her being gone from her Father's House, had been cast on her Reputation. And this appear'd so laudable a Wish, that she thought it would be an Indiscretion greater than any she had yet been guilty of, should she refuse it. She thought of nothing therefore but the manner in which she should consent, which she doubted not but he would ask at his next Coming to *Vincenza*.

I doubt not but the Reader will be pretty much surpris'd to find she could so easily be brought from one Extreme to another, and that she who but a few days before was all Despair and Rage, was already grown so temperate and calm; but there was a happy Instability in this Lady's Nature, which prevented her from anything for a long Time together; and it was this Disposition which carry'd her thro a Sea of innumerable Troubles, each of which would have been sufficient to have overwhelm'd another Woman. The Treachery with which her Confidence had been abus'd by *Florez*, the irreparable Injury her Virtue had received from the brutal Passion of *Ferdinand*, and the Grief which she was sensible the Loss of her was to her afflicted *Father*, were now no more remember'd, or consider'd only as Vexations which the gaining a Husband so meritous as *Henriquez* would amply compensate.

In Contemplations therefore, not displeasing, did she pass her Time; till about the third Day after the Departure of *Henriquez*, one of the Servants whom he had left to attend her, came running hastily into the Room where she was, and told her, That Don *Myrtano*, Brother to his Master, desir'd to speak with her. She cou'd have no Apprehensions of the true Reason of this Visit, and imagining only that some Accident having detain'd *Henriquez* longer than he design'd, he had commission'd him to tell her of it, went to receive him without any Concern, or Boding of the Miseries which this fatal Interview drew on her.

After the first Civilities were over, *Madam*, said he, *I have a Letter for you, which you ought to have receiv'd before; but the same unhappy Accident which delay'd the bringing it, has also been the Cause of my breaking it open; a Rudeness, I confess, which nothing but the Occasion could excuse.* In speaking these Words, he deliver'd a Paper to her, which was the same that *Henriquez* had writ to her the Moment before he fought with *Ferdinand*. The melancholy Air of his Deportment, and the Sighs which accompany'd his Expressions, gave her sufficient Reason to believe there was something extraordinary to be told her: But she suspended the latter Curiosity, to satisfy the greater, of knowing what this Letter contain'd; which opening hastily, she found in it these Lines:

To the Incomparable IDALIA

If anything were wanting to make my Charmer sensible of the Wonders of her Power, and the Effects it has wrought on me, what I am now about to acquaint her with, would be a Proof.

Don *Ferdinand*, either suspecting the Artifice which my Passion inspir'd me to deceive him with, or resenting the little

Care I seem'd to have of the Trust he repos'd in me, demands my Life for the Expiation of my Crime. I go this Moment to answer the Call of his Revenge, I cannot blame him; the Man who aims at so inestimable a Treasure as your Love, should, for that Blessing, quit all meaner Considerations; and in that View only it is, that I shall dare to maintain the Falsity I have told him, tho' at the Expence of my last Drop of Blood. But, as I am ignorant how, in this fatal Contest, Fate may deal with me, I snatch this Opportunity of pouring out a Million of soft, tender Wishes, while I give you this Assurance, that whatever is decreed for my Body, you wholly govern my immortal Part; the Sword of *Ferdinand* may pierce my Heart, but not eraze the bright *Idea* that my Soul is full of: When I am Ashes, the Passion you have inspir'd will have a Being; and living or dying I shall continue

Your Adorer,
HENRIQUEZ DE VELAGO

*Idalia* was too much interested in the Life of Don *Henriquez*, not to be impatient to hear the Issue of this Quarrel mention'd in the Letter; which being inform'd of by his Brother, she swoon'd away, o'ercome with Grief and Wonder. Don *Myrtano* was not idle in applying proper Means for her Recovery; which when he had effected, he began to entertain her in a very different Manner than what she cou'd have expected from so near a Relation to the Man who owed his Death to her malevolent Beauty: He was all Complaisance, all Gallantry, and seem'd so little astonish'd at what his Brother had done, that he assur'd her he should think a Death so caus'd more glorious than the longest Life, which gave not a Proof of being sensible of her Charms. This was indeed the Way to dissipate her Sorrows; but as she wanted not Wit nor Discernment, tho' her Vanity too often blinded her Judgment, she could not help thinking it a little odd that he should come there to visit her, and bring a Letter which he confessed he had taken the Liberty to open; and letting fall some Words which testify'd as much, he gave her to understand his Reasons for it, in this Manner: *I see, Madam*, said he, *that you are not more surprised at the Contents of this Letter, than that I am the Bearer of it; and because I should think it a Sin unpardonable to Heaven to oppose the Will of its most perfect Resemblance, the Divine* Idalia, *I shall endeavour to satisfy her, as far as in my Power, of every Particular of this unfortunate Adventure. Happening to be walking with your Father* Don Bernardo *on the Parade, the very Morning that he received a Letter from an unknown Hand, which gave him an Account of my Brother being bless'd with your Society, he desir'd me with the most earnest Conjurations to inform him what I knew of the Affair; to which I answer'd, as well I might, that I was so far from being let into any such Secret, that I verily believ'd it a Falsity; and when he spoke of coming to* Padua *in search of you, I offer'd to accompany him; which I had done, if not prevented by some Business which I could not put off. At his Return he sent for me, and seem'd concern'd that he had been guilty of wronging my Brother, and entreated me to make his Apology when next I saw him; which I told him would be in a short Time, and accordingly took Horse for* Padua *immediately. I alighted there at the very Moment that the Bodies of the two unhappy Rivals were brought in. The Consternation I was in, to see this dreadful Issue of a Friendship which promis'd a far different Consequence, can hardly be express'd: I stood for sometime without the Power of Speech, or Motion, and perhaps had not recover'd myself so soon, if a Servant, whom I knew to be the most favour'd one my Brother kept, had not rouz'd me from my Lethargy of Thought, by giving me a Paper, which he told me was writ by his Master, and put into his Hand, with a strict Charge to be deliver'd to a Lady at* Vicenza. *I was just about to carry it,* said he, *but am glad I made no greater Haste, since the Contents may possibly inform you the Reasons of this fatal Quarrel. In that Perplexity of Mind, I lost Decorum, and breaking the Seal, soon found the Fellow's Conjecture but too true,—that it was to* Love *I owed the Misfortune of my Brother's Death: Wonder not then, adorable* Idalia, (continu'd he, soft'ning his Voice,) *that I was fir'd with Impatience to behold a Beauty, whose Charms had given such a Proof of their prodigious Influence!—I come* (cry'd he, growing more tender) *to satisfy a Curiosity which, I fear, will cost me dear.* There was something so very graceful and engaging in the Air and Address of this young Gentleman, that it was almost impossible to see or hear him, without confessing a Sensibility of Perfections which very few, if any, could equal. *Idalia*, who had a Soul too capable of soft Impressions, full of warm Desires, and tender Languishments, tho' yet unfix'd, gaz'd on him with a Pleasure which as yet she knew not the Meaning of.—That Life and Gaiety which once had made her relish the Conversation of *Florez*,—that noble Mein and elegant Behaviour which had engag'd her Attention to the first Vows of *Ferdinand*,—and that submissive Tenderness which pleas'd her in the Addresses of *Henriquez*, and a thousand other different nameless

Graces, which seem'd united in the lovely *Myrtano*, inspir'd her, at the first Sight of him, with a Passion which she had neither Strength to repel, nor Artifice to conceal.—She now found in good Earnest what it was to love, and felt in reality those Emotions, which before she fancy'd to have done. He, who was perfectly acquainted with the Sex, and no Stranger to the Charms he had for 'em, immediately read it in her Eyes, and resolv'd to make his Advantage of it, in favour of those Desires, which few that saw *Idalia* but were possess'd with.

He staid not long at the *Villa*, after having entreated her to remain there his Guest, as she had been his Brother's, and to command everything in it with the same Freedom as she would do at Don *Bernardo's*; the necessary Preparations for the Funeral of *Henriquez*, whose Heir he was, obliging him to return to *Padua* with all Expedition. But the short Time he had been there, was sufficient to inspire the unhappy *Idalia* with such Sentiments as severely reveng'd the Destruction of his Brother.

The Infancy of Love is generally the most pleasing Part of it, when new Desires play round the innocent Heart, and gentle Thrillings warm the throbbing Veins, the tender Passion by swift, but unperceiv'd Degrees stealing thro' all the Seats of Life, affords only gay Wishes, pleasing Dreams, and rapturous Images of Joys to come; but in another manner did it enter the Soul of this unquiet Fair:—She no sooner found herself alone, than giving way to her impatient Passion, a thousand widely different Thoughts, all wild and stormy as a troubled Sea, o'erwhelm'd Reflection, and made Reason giddy:—She was presently sensible that she lov'd, and lov'd to that prodigious Height, that the least Appearance of an Obstacle to what she wish'd, was worse than Death: Her ruin'd Honour, and her blacken'd Fame seem'd now Misfortunes more terrible by far than ever they had done before. *Oh! 'tis impossible* (cry'd she to herself) *that* Myrtano, *the lovely, the accomplish'd* Myrtano, *can ever think the undone* Idalia *an Object worthy of his serious Affections!—No, 'twas all Gallantry!—all unmeaning Flattery which dictates the tender Words he spoke!—His Heart despises the Indiscretion of my Conduct!—Pity is the most tender Sentiment he can regard me with—And, oh! how distant is that from what I would inspire!* A Stream of Tears succeeded these Expressions: But this Passion having a little vented itself, the natural Vanity of her Disposition return'd to give the Consolation; and in this Humour she would say, *Yet why should I despair?—I am perhaps the only Person that judges with so much Severity of my Actions:* Henriquez *found enough in me to counterballance all that my Mismanagement has brought upon me, and why may I not hope his Brother may be of his Opinion?—My Eyes are still the same, and every Charm which us'd to attract, maintains its Lustre with unfading Brightness:—The Man to whom I ow'd my Shame, has with his Life repair'd the Injury he did me,—nor is my Birth unworthy of* Myrtano. With such kind of Sentiments would she a while beguile Despair; but then the excessive Eagerness with which she wish'd to appear amiable in the Eyes of this Charmer of her Soul, suggested another Difficulty which she knew not how to get over.—*Fool that I am,* (resum'd she,) *and too liable to entertain the vain Delusions of fictitious Hope:—'Tis not in Nature,—'tis not in Reason, to expect the Man whose Brother I have kill'd, should love me:—The noble* Henriquez, *but for me, might have liv'd long and happily;—for my curs'd Sake he dy'd, and* Myrtano *is bound to hate me;—should he forgive it, the Ghost of that unhappy Youth would rise to blast us in the midst of Rapture!—O Torture! Horror! Hell!—it cannot,— must not be,—both Heaven and Earth forbid it!—*Henriquez *cannot be recall'd, and* Myrtano *must not love:*

In Agonies not to be express'd, not to be *conceiv'd* but by the Heart that felt 'em, did this half-distracted Lady pass the Night after the Departure of *Myrtano*; but the Morning brought her a Comforter beyond her Hopes: She was scarce risen from the Bed, which the Confusion of her Thoughts had made most restless, when she receiv'd a Letter, which opening with a Mixture of Delight and Pain, as believing it came from him who had the sole Power of bestowing either, she read these Lines:

To the Never-enough-admir'd
IDALIA

It is not the bleeding Body of my only Brother, yet uninterr'd, it is not the Apprehensions how, at so unfit a Season, you may condemn my rash Proceeding, can deter me from making a Declaration as suitable to your Beauty, as it is the contrary to my present Circumstance. But you were created only to work Wonders, and in the midst of Death and Horror disclose an opening Heaven, whose Brightness will suffer no other Ideas but itself to appear in the Remembrance.

The Curiosity which Yesterday brought me to *Vicenza*, has involv'd me in a Passion which must render me either the most blest, or the most wretched of Mankind. Who loves *Idalia* can

have no Medium in his Fate; what then must be the Terrors of
Suspence in an Affair on which depends far more than Life?
Ease them, I conjure you, most adorable *Idalia*! and either send
me to the Grave with my unhappy Brother, or permit me to
live in the felicitous Hope of being one Day

Yours,<br>Myrtano De Velago

P.S. Whether you pardon or condemn the Presumption of
this, let a Line inform me: If the *former*, expect me to return
Thanks at your Feet, as soon as the Obsequies of my Brother
are perform'd; if the *latter*, to hear I am no more.

With what Transports of unbounded Joy she read these Words,
let those be judge who love like her: A thousand, thousand Times
she kiss'd the dear, the welcome Mandate; then put it to her Heart,
repeating to herself the ravishing Contents;—then snatch'd it out again,
as loth to lose the Sight of what had given her so infinite a Satisfaction,
that scarce the Author of it, had he been present, could have added to
it; the Extasy so fill'd her Soul, that she thought not of answering it,
till a Servant inform'd her the Messenger, who brought it, waited to
be dispatch'd. He shall not long, *(cry'd she, starting as it were from some
delightful Dream,)* and immediately running to a Table whereon stood a
Standish, made him this Reply:

To Don Myrtano

In what Manner can a Person so much oblig'd receive an
Overture of Love, without appearing guilty either of an
Indecorum to *herself*, or Ingratitude to *you*? If I accept too
readily of the Heart you offer, how shall I answer it to the
Modesty of my Sex? And if I reject it, what way is left
for me to repay the many Favours I am indebted for?—
Severe Necessity! that whichsoever Path I tread, it leads
to Condemnation;—yet such is the Cruelty of my Fate! I
therefore will chuse neither, but remain unbyas'd till Time,
and a more perfect Acquaintance with your Humour, shall
inform me what will best become *Bernardo's* Daughter

Idalia

ELIZA HAYWOOD

P.S. While I am a welcome Guest at *Vicenza*, I shall expect you to tell me so, as frequently as you can.

It was with all the Difficulty in the World she restrain'd herself from writing with more Tenderness, and when she read over what she was about to send, it appeared so cold, and so far unlike the sincere Dictates of her Wishes, that she could not forbear adding a Postscript, for fear he should imagine her, indeed, altogether insensible of his Merit, and give over the hopeless Prosecution; nor was she reconciled to what she had done till the next Morning, much about the same Hour she had received the former, she was agreeably disturb'd from her Sleep by a second *Billet*, the Contents of which were these:

To the Adorable IDALIA

The Sight of your dear Hand gave me a Joy too exquisite to be allay'd, even by the cold Reluctance with which you seem to treat a Passion the sincerest that ever *Man* profess'd, or *Woman* welcom'd. Methinks there shou'd need no more to convince you of the Power of your triumphant Charms, than two such Victims as *Ferdinand* and *Henriquez*; and whenever you doubt my Truth, it cannot be that you call in question your own Beauty, but my Incapacity of distinguishing it:—But Time, (as you are pleased to say,) as it will *convince* you, so I hope will also move you to *compassionate* what is felt by

Your most Faithful Slave,<br>MYRTANO DE VELAGO

P.S. The Body of the unfortunate *Henriquez* is this Night to be reposited in the Tomb of his Ancestors, and I hope Tomorrow's Evening will bring me to *Vicenza*.—Prepare, if possible, to receive me with a Smile, lest I envy the Condition of him I leave behind me, and regret a Life made miserable by your Displeasure.

There was not Abundance of Occasion for this Pressure in the Postscript; the enamour'd *Idalia* would have found it a difficult Task to have dress'd her Face in Frowns whenever he appear'd, had she never so much endeavour'd it; and she was so much an Enemy to disguising her Sentiments, that he might easily read them in the Answer which she return'd. It was in this Manner:

To Don MYRTANO

If I were not willing to harbour a Thought so entirely disagreeable to my own Desires, I should imagine there was more of Raillery than Sincerity in the Declaration your first Letter made me. I am not so little conscious of my own Demerits, as to believe myself capable of inspiring a Passion such as you describe;—but I shall make Allowances for that: I am sensible you Men of Wit know how to *magnify*,—and if I have not the better Opinion of the small Share of Beauty I am Mistress of, I shall most certainly of your Elegance, in raising an *Idea* so infinitely beyond what it is in Reality.—All I wish is, that in good earnest you may talk yourself into an Imposition on your own Judgment, and never see more than now you seem to do, the Faults of

IDALIA

P.S. I shall impatiently expect you Tomorrow at *Vicenza*, and shall take care not to wear a Countenance too melancholy, lest it should remind you (more than will be for my Advantage) of our common Loss in the generous *Henriquez*:—Till then,—Adieu.

In Contemplations much the same as she had entertain'd herself with the Night before, did she pass this. The ensuing Day slid on insensibly, while she was employ'd in studying Airs, and practising in her Glass new Graces, to make the already-charm'd *Myrtano* more enflamed. At length he came, and whether the extraordinary Desire each had to please, or that (as most People at some Times look more aimable than at others) that Day they chanced to do so. But the before too potent Charms of both, seem'd improv'd at this second View: The sparkling Eyes of *Myrtano*, which before shone with Amazement at the uncommon Beauties they beheld in *Idalia's*, had now a tender Languor,—a swimming Extacy,—a soft, beseeching, nameless, Loveliness, mix'd with their Lustre, and spake without the Help of Words, the Wishes of his Soul. The Mourning Dress he had on set off to vast Advantage the Delicacy of his Complection, which was of so unmatch'd a Whiteness, that there required all that Majesty and Loftiness of Mien, which in his Whole Deportment shew'd itself to keep him from Effeminacy; and, indeed, never did Nature unite such contrary Perfections with so engaging a Harmony as in his Composition: A *distant* View shew'd him all *Hero*, adorn'd with every manly martial Grace, and inspired Awe in the admiring Gazer; but his *near* Approach dissolv'd in softning Languishments the Soul, and spoke him form'd for all the Joys of *Love*. Thus, but far more enchanting than Description can have Power to represent him, did he appear to the transported *Idalia;* but that the Reader may have some little Notion of his Charms, take the Idea of 'em set down by her who best knew how to paint them.

The Character of MYRTANO; writ by
IDALIA, and found afterwards in her
Closet.

*Bright, lovely, graceful, are all Words below*
*What to Myrtano's Character we owe:*
*Divinely glorious! Godlike! speaks but Part!*
*He yet has Charms which nearer touch the Heart!*
*These, awful Wonder, and our Homage claim,*
*But there's a Sweetness Language cannot name:*
*A Soul-enchanting Softness, (far above*
*The Reach of Thought, unknowing him to prove)*
*Dwells in his Air, amidst his Glories plays*
*And tempers, not diminishes the Blaze.*

*Here* Fancy *stoops to court the Aid of Sense,*
*Unable to conceive such Excellence!*
*Imagination may a Form create*
*Correctly Lovely, and supremely Great;*
*But, Oh! how mean would that* Idea *be*
*To what, indeed, is to be found in* Thee!
*Joy-mingled Wonder kindles at thy Sight*
*And clothes our Admiration with Delight.*

*As Tapers languish at th' Approach of Day*
*And by degrees melt slow their Shine away;*
*A while they glimmer with contracted Spires*
*Trembling, unable to relax their Fires:*
*But when the Sun's broad Eye is open'd wide*
*And Beams, thick flashing, shoot on every Side;*
*No more their emulative Force they try*
*But quite o'erwhelmed with Radiance sink, and die;*
*So those pale Lights, whose Glare late shar'd our Praise*
*Are wholly lost in thy Almighty Blaze.*
*Eraz'd and blotted from the Book of* Fame.
*Her thousand Tongues swell with thy charmful Name:*
*No other* Sound *now strikes our ravish'd* Ears,
*No other* Form *in our glad* View *appears;*
*So fully o'er the Soul thy Influence reigns*
*That not one Rebel-Thought thy Sway disdains.*

Had the Lover of *Idalia* been as Poetically inclined, 'tis possible we might have had a better Description of her transmitted to Posterity, than I am able to gather from the imperfect Accounts I received from those who gave me the History of her Life; but since that has not been done, everybody is at liberty to form an *Idea* of what appears most pleasing to them; for that she was one of the most lovely of her Sex, is evident from that prodigious Power of charming, which gain'd her almost as many Admirers, as they had Eyes to gaze upon her.

But to return to her Conversation with *Myrtano:*—It was such as was agreeable to their Characters; all Wit, all Elegance, all Tenderness, and Love: They were equally transported with each other, and 'tis hard to say which had the better in this Race of Passion. *Idalia*, indeed, testified her's no other Way than in list'ning with a pleas'd Attention to his Vows; but there needed no more to make the happy Lover consider her as half obtain'd already, and tho' he did not immediately press for the Gratification of his Wishes, he did not in the least despair. He made her several Visits, in which nothing happen'd of any greater Consequence than to increase her Admiration of him. She never saw him without discovering some new Perfection; and that Height of Passion with which she at last regarded him, would be injured by an ordinary Lover's Imagination of it: But notwithstanding the rapturous Reflection of being beloved by a Man who appear'd so every Way meritorious, she had pretty near as equal a Share of Disquiet, that he had never in all his Solicitations mention'd the least Word of Marriage. A thousand, and a thousand Times he had told her, That he lived but in her Sight:—That he should court Death as a Blessing, if any Accident should deprive him of her:—That the united Charms of her whole Sex besides, would be ineffectual to alienate his Thoughts one Moment from her;—and swore as many Vows of an eternal Constancy, as there were Saints in Heaven to witness 'em. She knew he aim'd with an abounded Ardor to possess her, but knew not by what Way he wish'd to do so; and this, whenever it came cross her Thoughts, embitter'd all the Sweetness of his Love, and shook'd her to the Soul. She resolved at length to summon all her Courage, to say something to him which should oblige him to discover what his Intentions were; and she had no sooner fix'd herself in a Determination to do so, than she found she had more Cause for it than before she had been sensible of.

There are Times when even the most Prudent are not Masters of their Actions; how then could it be expected that the Young, Gay, Enflamed *Myrtano* should have always the Power of commanding his, in Opportunities such as he enjoy'd: As yet, indeed, he never had transgressed the strictest Rules of Decency; but *Desire* becoming, by Restraint, more fierce, at last grew wild, and would no longer endure to be controul'd by dull Respect.

He never came to *Vicenza*, but he staid a Night or two: A little Room adjoining *Idalia's* Chamber was that in which they generally supp'd together, and seldom parted early. As they were entertaining each other on the usual Theme, and mingling Kisses with their Vows of Passion, by some Accident his Sleeve catching hold of a Corner of a Table on which the Lights were set, he threw it down: What Lover is not fond of Darkness? The impatient *Myrtano* bless'd the happy Chance; and thinking this the lucky Moment ordain'd to give him all his Soul at present long'd for, he snatch'd the trembling Fair, and easily finding his Way into the next Room, bore her to the Bed, and was pretty near the Accomplishment of his Desires, before the Surprise she was in, at this sudden Change of his Behaviour, could permit her to make any Resistance; but when she did, it was so strenuously, that without being guilty of the same Violence as *Ferdinand* had been, it was impossible for him to proceed. In spite of all the tender Passion with which she had regarded him,—in spite of the secret Inclinations which, perhaps, at this very Instant work'd very strongly within her in his

Favour,—in spite of all his Tears, his Prayers, his Vows, her *Virtue* got the better, and triumph'd o'er *Desire*. But tho' she had *gain'd* with such unequal Arms a Conquest so truly glorious, she could not assure herself of *maintaining* it; nor would consent to pardon his Attempt, but on Condition he would leave her, and retire that Moment to his own Appartment. He, who was not of a Humour apt to despond, and had a real Passion for her, thought it best to comply, not doubting but a second Endeavour might prevail on her to *bestow* what he found he could not now obtain but by *Force*.

But his Behaviour had wrought a quite different Effect on the Mind of *Idalia* than he imagin'd:—She had already suffer'd too much by that unruly Passion, which goes by the Mistaken Name of *Love*, to think the Man who took the same Measures had any other Design than to ruin her; and the Racks that she endured in endeavouring to vanquish a Tenderness which she had so much Reason to believe an Enemy to her Honour, were past the Reach of Thought. Resolving, however, to be certain of the Truth of what she fear'd, she put in Execution the Design she before had form'd; and as soon as she saw him come into her Chamber the next Morning, plucking up all the Courage she was Mistress of, she saluted him in this Manner: *The Confusion I was in last Night*, said she, *took from me the Power of resenting, as I ought, the mean Opinion your Behaviour testified you have of my Virtue. I had too entire a Confidence in your Honour to imagine you were capable of harbouring a Thought to my Prejudice; but as you have shew'd me the Error I was guilty of, I shou'd indeed deserve Contempt, cou'd I consent to remain longer under a Roof where the Master of it makes so ill a Use of the Power my fond Belief has given him.*—It was to no purpose that he endeavour'd to qualify the Bitterness of these Reproaches, by all the tender Expressions he was able; for perceiving he was yet far from making that Offer which alone could convince her he meant her fair, she grew more sensibly enraged; and now bent to try him to the utmost, *Speak no more, Don* Myrtano, resumed she, *the Man that wou'd* dishonour *me can never* love *me.*—*'Tis brutal Passion, not sincere Affection, that acts as you have done. Did you, indeed, believe me worthy of the Tenderness you so well can feign,* Respect *had govern'd* Appetite, *and fetter'd* loose *Desire:*—*All Wishes, all Inclination wou'd have been stifled till the Church's Sanction had made it lawful:*—*But I perceive, too late for my Repose,* (continued she, bursting into Tears,) *that I am fallen too low for such a Hope.* She spoke no more for sometime, both in Expectation of his Answer, and to indulge a few Sighs, which the Suppression of had made uneasy to her. But he was too much confounded at her last Words to be able to return an immediate Answer to 'em: He loved her indeed with a Transcendency of Passion, but there were many Reasons which oppos'd his marrying her; it being wholly improper, however, for him to tell her so, he artfully evading the Question, turn'd the Discourse on the unbounded Force of Love, and how little it was in the Power of a Person possess'd with it, to repel the most unexcusable Instigations of it. But *Idalia* perceiving, with an Infinity of Grief and Vexation, the Deceit, would not be so put off; and in plain Terms assured him this should be the last Moment of his seeing her, unless he gave her some convincing Proof he had no other Intentions than what would be consistent with her Honour to approve of. Not all his Wit, not all his perswasive Eloquence, than which never Man had more, could furnish him with Expressions prevalent enough to occasion the least Alteration in her Humour:— She still insisted on the Article of Marriage; and he was at last obliged to confess that there were some Particulars in his Circumstances which as yet she was ignorant of, that made it impossible for him to answer her Demands in the Manner she desired at present. He palliated, however, the Bitterness of this Reply with ten thousand Protestations of eternal Love, and giving her a solemn Oath, that in a few Days she should be satisfy'd in everything, engaged a Promise from her not to leave *Vicenza* till he return'd.

Here was now an Alteration in the Fate of this distracted Lady: She thought herself the most wretched of created Beings; all that can be conceived of Shame, Despair, Grief, Rage, and Horror, is short of what she felt in this Disappointment of her high-rais'd Hopes:—She lov'd, she lov'd to Madness a Man who she was now too sensible aim'd only at her Dishonour; and yet she was obliged to him; was still under his Roof; and what was worse, in the cruel Necessity of either still remaining so, or returning to *Venice*, the Thought of which was Death, after the Notice her late Adventures had made there.—O the Severity of the Struggle, when *Love* and *Virtue* are at Variance, and rend the divided Soul with equal Fury!—Yet such was her Condition; and, unable entirely to vanquish the Efforts of *either*, by Turns took part with *both*; and, 'tis uncertain whether wholly following the Emotions of her impatient Passion, she at last had not yielded to be *Myrtano's* on any Terms, or, guided by the other, had not resolved to quit his House, and fly the Danger which so imminently threaten'd her if she staid, if in the midst of her Distraction she had not receiv'd a Letter which at once determined her Resolve. It came to her the next Day after *Myrtano* had taken Leave of her; and the Contents, which were written in an unknown Hand, were these:

To Donna *Idalia de Bellsache*

If your Willingness to believe, has not already rendered the Caution I would give you ineffectual, this may prevent the Ruin which is design'd for you.

My Intimacy with Don *Myrtano* has not only drawn from him the Secret of your being log'd at his *Villa*, but also of the Professions he has made you. As you, perhaps, are ignorant of his Engagements with the Niece of Count *Miramont*, you may with the greater Ease be brought to credit what he says:—But after the Knowledge of it, it will, to the Punishment the Crime itself will draw upon you, add that of the Contempt of the whole World, should you persist to listen to his Vows.—In time, most lovely *Idalia*, retire from a Place which is design'd the Scene of your Ruin.—The vain, gay, inconstant *Myrtano* thinks no Woman worthy of a serious Passion:—And as Interest is the greatest Motive of his *Marriage*, so to triumph over the Weakness of your Sex, is the only Inducement to his Endeavours of adding to the Number of those his Protestations have undone, the credulous *Idalia.*—I have no other Interest in giving you this Advice, than to save *you* the Shame and Misery of a too-late Repentance, and my *Friend* the Sin of having occasion'd it:— What use you make of it, I shall be informed by him, who will not be at the Pains of concealing anything he accounts so trivial as an Amour, such as he is entring into with you.—Be kind, therefore, to yourself, fly his destructive Charms; and when you have escaped the Snare, shall know who was

Your Adviser

This was enclosed in another Paper, on which was writ these Lines:

Since I writ the Enclosed, I hear by Don *Myrtano,* that, apprized of his ungenerous Dealing, you design to quit his House; if it really be your Intention, you ought to have conceal'd it, since he resolves to take the effectual Measures to secure you there, at least, till, by Force or Insinuation, he has obtained a Gratification of his Desires.—which he tells me shall be delay'd no longer than a few Days.

As passionately enamour'd as *Idalia* was, she had a Stock of Haughtiness, which nothing could surmount; and her *Pride* receiving as severe a Shock by this Intelligence as her *Virtue*, it entirely turn'd the Scale, and weigh'd down *Love—'s Death!* said she to herself, *dare he presume to think thus meanly of me?—Sollicited for a* Prostitute, *while in the mean Time his serious Vows are address'd to another!—O Torture! What has the Niece of* Miramont *to boast superior to the Daughter of* Bernardo?—*False!—stupid!—blind!—ungrateful Traytor!—But I'll not endure it!—Daggers or Poisons shall revenge me!—I'll murder him, and then myself!* In this Manner did she rave, till almost breathless with the swelling Passion, she'd stop, and read the fatal Scroll again; and coming to that Part of it which mention'd that this unknown *Adviser* had his Intelligence from *Myrtano* himself,—*Hell and Confusion*, cry'd she out, *the Villain has expos'd me too!—My easy Nature, and my fond Belief is Food for the base Mirth of all his lewd Companions!—Every tender Folly,—each unguarded Languishment betray'd and ridicul'd! Distraction! Can I live, and suffer it!*—Then contemplating further on what she had read,—*But yet*, resum'd she, *this is the least of Ills, that is already done, the Monster threatens me with more and greater. Oh! whither shall I turn to escape?* As she was employ'd in these perplex'd Meditations, a Servant that us'd to attend her in her Chamber, who was by Nature extremely violent in all her Passions, and had taken the least Pains to vanquish 'em, could not contain herself before this Creature; and Jealousy being the uppermost Emotion of her Soul, she presently enquir'd if she knew the Niece of Count *Miramont:* To which the Wench having answer'd that she did,—*And is she handsome?* cry'd the other impatiently. *To an infinite Degree*, said the cunning Creature: *Heaven never made a Face more beautiful, except your own.—No Flattery*, resum'd *Idalia, I am not in a Humour to receive it.—But if you would oblige, inform me of all you know concerning the intended Marriage between that Lady and you Master: Ardella*, so she was call'd, affected a prodigious Surprise at these Words, and suffer'd herself to be ask'd a hundred Times before she made any Reply; and when she did, it was in such a Manner as gave no

Satisfaction. This Behaviour put *Idalia* almost beside herself; she was perswaded that she knew more than she was willing to reveal; and, wild with the Uncertainty, pray'd, promis'd, threaten'd, and accompany'd all she said with such Pressures, that the other appear'd mov'd by 'em, and at last confessed, That her Master was indeed to be married to that Lady; that everything was at that very Time preparing for their Nuptials;—and that never were two Persons more passionately charm'd with each other than they appear'd to be.—*But*, Madam, added she with a well-counterfeited Fear, *should you reveal the least Syllable of what I have told you, to my Master, I am certain he wou'd not let me live an Hour.—Trouble not yourself,* cry'd *Idalia,* interrupting her, *I never more will see him.—No,* continued she, raising her Voice, and stamping, *I call just Heaven, and every Saint to witness, I never will consent to see or hear him more:—Too much already have I listned to his perjur'd Vows;—which, when I do again, may all the Plagues of Earth and Hell fall on me:—May I be ruin'd, then thrown off to scorn,—driven round the World with no Companion by my Infamy, and not one Friend to pity, or relieve me, till some unlook'd for horrid kind of Death o'ertakes me, and sinks my Soul, with all its Load of Guilt, beyond the reach of Mercy.*—A thousand such like Imprecations did she make; but where to go to avoid the Penalty of them, she was for a good while undetermined. At last she remember'd to have heard of a *Monastery* at *Verona,* which being a Place she was utterly unknown at, she made choice of: It was there she design'd to fix, knowing it would be easy for her, immediately after she was introduc'd, to write to her Father for a Supply of Money, against the Time of her being initiated; for she was now in the Mind to leave the World forever. She could not think of quitting *Myrtano's* House without the Knowledge of *Ardella,* and therefore communicated to her what her Intentions were; to which she, with a seeming Reluctance, consented, and promis'd to order Things for her Departure, with that Secrecy, that no other Servant in the Family should have any Suspicion of it.

All the necessary Preparations for her little Journey being made, by Break of Day she left *Vicenza;* but with what Heart-Akings, those who, like her, have tore themselves from all that's dear, can best be judge. At her Departure she gave a Letter to *Ardella,* with a pressing Entreaty to deliver it to *Myrtano:* It was full of Upbraidings, mix'd with Tenderness, and express'd in so moving a Manner the Anguish of her Soul, that it was scarce possible for a Heart which had ever known the Force of Love, to read it without melting; and perhaps, even in the midst of her

Indignation, was not without a Wish that it might bring him after her to *Verona.*—She had still Remains enough of Vanity to desire to have him in her power, tho' she had made so solemn a Vow never to make any other Use of it, than to disdain and hate him.

But what befel her in her Way to *Verona*, and the vast Variety of surprising Incidents which ensu'd each other thro' the whole Course of her unhappy Life, I must defer till another Opportunity; having already spun out the *Beginning* of her Misfortunes to such a Length, that the *Continuance* of them would give me a just Apprehension of becoming *tiresome* to those I endeavour to *divert.*

*The End of the First Part*

# Part II

With no other Companions than her own disturb'd Meditations, and one Man, whom Don *Myrtano's* Servant-Maid had provided for her as a Guide, did the sorrowful *Idalia* quit the House of her Beloved. They had not travell'd many Hours, before she found herself in a Place suited, as it were, by Nature to her present Disposition: It was a Forest, wild and desolate; the trackless Paths discover'd not that any human Feet had ever trod them.—No Fields of Corn, no Vines, no Olives here were planted; no limpid Streams, no cool refreshing Rivulets appeared to charm the Eye with gay delightful Prospects, and with their pleasing Murmurs sooth the list'ning Ear; but sapless Trees, whose wind-bent, Leafless Twigs hung quivering to oppose the Traveller's Passage, and rank and unwholsome Weeds unfit for Use, hemm'd in the Borders of some stagnate Brooks, which here and there, by Length of Time, the falling Rains had made, composed a sad unbless'd Variety, and spread an *Area* of nought but Horror. The deep *Revery* she was in, which the melancholy Solitude of everything about her had indulg'd, prevented her from taking any notice how improbable it was that this should be a Road, especially such a one as that of consequence must be, which led to *Verona*, than which no Town in *Italy* was more frequented: But they were not enter'd into it above some two or three hundred Paces, before the Man, appointed to conduct her, stopping his Horse, obliged her to do so too; and looking on her with a Countenance between stern and troubled, *Madam*, said he, *what think you of this Place? Does it not seem cut out for Rapes and Murders, and every Act of Horror?* These Words, and the Manner in which they were spoke, was sufficient to rouze *Idalia* from that Lethargy of Thought she had been in, and wake her into Terror, *Cou'd I believe my Life were an Offence*, reply'd she, *or were I conscious of any Action which shou'd excite Revenge, I might, indeed, suspect that I shou'd find it here.—Innocence*, resum'd he, *is not alway a Protection.—You have, perhaps, incur'd more Displeasure than you are sensible of;—for what Cause, is not my Business to examine, but I have received a Reward to put an end to your Misfortunes by this*—With these last Words he shew'd her a Dagger, which he had wore conceal'd under his Riding-Coat. As much as *Idalia* had threaten'd to do a Violence on herself, as much as she thought Life a Burden, ruin'd in her Fortune and Reputation, disappointed in her Love, and depriv'd of everything the World calls dear, the Imagination she was so near Death, made her Soul shake with Agonies unfelt before: She burst into a Flood of Tears, and throwing herself at his Feet, conjur'd him to spare her, in Terms so soft, so moving, so perswasive, that the Heart which had deny'd, must have been more than savage: The most harden'd and accustom'd Murderer must have relented at such a pity-moving Object, and dropp'd the Dagger, if not turn'd the Point against himself, for having thus alarm'd her.—What then became of him whose Sentiments, however he appear'd at present, were full of Honour, and scorn'd so base, so barbarous a Deed. Tears started from his Eyes, and his whole Frame seem'd convuls'd with inward Tremblings, *Rise, Madam, rise,* (said he, as soon as he had Power to speak,) *and, if you can, forgive the Terror I have caus'd, and for which I am ready to expire with Grief and Penitence.— But, to convince you, I never had a Thought to execute the bloody Purpose I presum'd to threaten, I have provided you a Place where you may remain in Safety, which 'tis impossible you can do at* Verona. The blooming Colour which had so lately forsook the Cheeks of the afrighted *Fair*, return'd, at this Assurance, with all its wonted Beauty; and looking more earnestly than she had done before on this Person whose Behaviour had given her such different Emotions, she could easily perceive, tho' his Garb was mean, his Air, and the Address with which he pronounced these last Words, were far from that of a *Ruffian*. She imagin'd also, that she saw something in his Face which was not unknown to her; but when or how she had been acquainted with it, was out of her Power to recollect.

After she had testified the Sense she had of his obliging Offer by some Expressions of Gratitude, she desired to be inform'd of what he knew concerning the Inhumanity intended against her, and who they were that persecuted her with such a causeless Malice. To which, after a little Pause, he replied in this Manner: *'Tis easy for you, Madam,* said he, *to guess that* Ardella *had her Share in the abhorr'd Design, because you know very well that it was by her I was appointed your Conductor; and I shall make no Scruple to confess that it was from her Mouth I received my Orders to dispatch you, and from her Hand my Hire, which was, indeed, a Sum too great for a Creature of her Station to bestow, and, if she had not told me, that by performing her Injunction I should oblige a powerful Friend, would have made me know it must be to a Person of the highest Rank I owed it.* 'Twould be impossible to represent the Consternation *Idalia* was in at hearing these Words: An Imagination came immediately into her Head more dreadful to her than the Death she had escaped; and lifting up her Eyes, streaming a second Time with Tears, *O too well*, (cried she,) *too well I understand you!* Myrtano's *Servant could not reach the Price of such an Undertaking; but* Myrtano's *self might well afford it.*—*Oh! 'tis he*,—*'tis he*, (pursu'd she, in an Agony which was not far off Distraction,) *the false, ungrateful, perjur'd Man! Conscious of Guilt, and taught by my Behaviour how much I scorn'd to aid his brutal Raptures, the Passion he avow'd is turn'd to Hate!*—*Engaged to another, and unable to perform what Honour did require, my Death alone could silence my Upbraidings! Cruel Reward for Love! Inhuman Policy!*—*Barbarous* Myrtano!—

In these and many more the like Complainings did she pour out the Anguish of her Soul, without any Regard of the Person who was witness of them; nor would he interrupt her, being willing to be let into the whole Affair between her and *Myrtano*, till perceiving she was silent, *Tho' for many Reasons, Madam*, said he, *Don* Myrtano *is the man in the world I least esteem, yet I cannot suffer you to continue in this Opinion, without being guilty of an Injustice I could not answer to myself.*—Myrtano, *Madam, I dare swear, is perfectly innocent of any Design against your* Life:—*What he may have form'd against your* Honour, *yourself is the best Judge.*

He said no more, waiting to hear in what Manner she would reply; but tho' the Alteration of her Looks and Gestures sufficiently testified the Effect his Words had wrought in her, she forbore to speak how much she rejoic'd to find *Myrtano* guiltless of the Crime she had just now suspected him of, and probably imagining he might also be so of everything he had been accus'd of, conjur'd her kind Informer to acquaint her if there were anything of Truth in the Report, that he was to be marry'd to the Niece of Count *Miramount*; which he assuring her that there was, and that the Nuptials were to be solemniz'd so suddenly, that all the necessary Preparations for the Magnificence of it were as good as finish'd, made her again relapse into her former Violence of Temper.

*Then he is a Traytor still*, (cry'd she, transported at once with Grief and Indignation,) *and is guilty of a worse Crime than conspiring against my Life could be:*—*My Peace of Mind, my everlasting Quiet he has destroy'd,*—*expos'd,*—*betray'd me to a Rival's Scorn!*—*'s Death! to pretend Courtship to me, at the very Time he was solliciting another,*—*the same insinuating Looks,*—*the same dissembled Tenderness,*—*the same undoing Vows address'd to both at once!*—*Was ever Man so base?* She had run on with a great deal more of the same Nature, if he had not put a Stop to

ELIZA HAYWOOD

her, by telling her, That whatever Reason she had to condemn *Myrtano*, his intended Bride had certainly an equal Share, who lov'd as much, and was as much deceiv'd:—*Nay, infinitely more,* (added he) *in my Opinion, since, had not her Quality been too great for him to hazard such a Breach, you had doubtless had the Preference in all Things, as well as in his Affections.* Notwithstanding the solemn Vow *Idalia* had made never to see him more, she could not be told anything which flatter'd the Tenderness she had for him, without feeling a secret Pleasure; and having enter'd into a Discourse of the Lady design'd to be his Wife, she ask'd a thousand Questions concerning her Wit, Beauty, and Humour; for this envy'd Fair having been brought up from her Infancy at *Rome* with her Uncle Count *Miramount*, and but lately come to *Venice*, she had never happen'd to see her; but her jealous Curiosity receiv'd but little Satisfaction in this Point, there appear'd in the Person she enquir'd of, a great Unwillingness to make any Answers to such Interrogatories; and to put an End to them, he reminded her, that if she design'd to go to that little *Asylum* he had provided for her, it was high Time to begin their Journey, it being a good many Miles distant from the Place they were now in. She readily acquiesc'd, and that Evening about Sun-set arriv'd at a neat, but small Dwelling, such as the Poet describes to be the Abode of *Baucis* and *Philemon*: A good old Man and Woman, pretty near the same Age, came forth to welcome her, and, while her Guide was employ'd in taking Care of his Horses, conducted her in, and shew'd her to a Chamber, which, tho' it could boast no Finery, was extremely clean and decent, and had everything in it fit to charm a contemplative Mind. The Windows were cover'd with *Fillaree* and *Jessamine*, only where here and there Spaces were cut to give the Eye a most delightful Prospect o'er distant Meadows, Fields, and Vineyards; a sweet Confusion *without* fill'd the while rural Scene, and fed extensive Thought with all the Charms of Nature:—*Within*, a vast Variety of collected Books, and choicest Maps, brought to the View the spacious Universe, improving Reason with the Aids of *Art*.

Idalia, whose Wishes at this Time were dead to all the noisy Splendor of a Town, seem'd perfectly pleas'd with it, and told her Hosts she should think it the greatest Blessing Life could now afford her, to be permitted to spend the Remainder of her Days with them in that agreeable Retirement. While she was speaking, he who had brought her there, came into the Room, and took upon him to answer what she had been saying in this Manner: *I am highly satisfy'd, Madam,* said he, *that there is anything which can make you wish a Confinement here, so long as is necessary for your Safety; but can never consent, that after that Time you should deprive the World of its most valuable Ornament:—* No, no, (continued he very respectfully,) *you must again shine out the Star of* Venice, *adorn'd by all who gaze upon you, and resume that native Lustre which the Baseness of Mankind has for a while has eclips'd, but never can extinguish.—O talk of it no more,* (interrupted she,) *I never will return to* Venice. *What! to see the History of my Misfortunes writ in the Smiles of every Face that meets me!—to endure the stinging Satire, the Reflections which all the Friends of* Ferdinand *and* Henriques *will throw upon me!—and that worst Curse, the Scorn of that too happy hated she, who soon, you say,* Myrtano *must call Wife!—O no! I cannot bear it!—ruin'd in all my Hopes, and past the Power of even Heaven itself to make my Woes less terrible, I'll hide 'em ever from the unpitying World, and die alone unknown, and unlamented. Were your Condition so desperate as you imagine,* (resum'd he,) *I know not if I should perswade you to return; but there may be, perhaps, a Way found out to bring you to your Father's Arms with as much Honour as when you left them, and raise you above the Rage or the Disdain of all whom you call Enemies. Oh! forbear,* (said she, unwilling to give way to a Hope of anything which seem'd so much an Impossibility,) *forbear, obliging Stranger! to turn my Thoughts back on the Scene of my past Happiness or sooth Imagination with such idle Flattery of what's to come.—Can e'er the Days of Innocence return?—Can my polluted Honour e'er be cleans'd from the vile Stain it bears?—Can I again appear a Virgin?—Racking Reflections!—Why do you rouze them in me?—Why, after such Proofs of Generosity and Pity, do you alarm Remembrance with these dread Ideas, to make Thought sick, the Light grow hateful to me, and that Life you gave scarce worthy my Thanks. Far be if from me,* (answer'd he, bowing,) *to renew the Memory of what may be distasteful; but I would fain perswade you to believe, that Heaven, which has so miraculously preserv'd your Life, will also make it happy.—Surprising Things by a Hand unseen are often brought to pass: When you left* Myrtano's *House, you little suspected that the Person appointed for your* Guide, *was design'd to be your* Murderer: *Nor did they, who brib'd me to that excrable Deed, imagine how distant my Thoughts were from such an Undertaking:—Why then should you not hope, that by some Turn of Fate, as strange and unexpected, you may again be bless'd.—Oh! 'tis impossible!* (cry'd the uneasy *Idalia.*) *Suppose* (resum'd the other hastily) *your Beauty, in spite of all has happen'd, should charm a Man whose Quality and Fortune you could have no Objections to, the*

*Title of his Wife would silence Calumny, restore your Fame, and make you thought as happy as he'd be truly bless'd. If such an Offer* (reply'd she, in a haughty Air) *ever should occur, he must have more than Quality and Fortune to recommend him to my Esteem: Fallen as I am, I would be lower yet, rather than sell my Liberty for sordid Interest, and the World's Opinion.—No, no, tho' lost to all besides, I still am Mistress of myself,—my own unconquerable Will!*—Idalia *can be by nought but Inclination subdued; and that, alas!* (pursued she, softening her Voice,) *is lavish'd all on the too-lovely, false* Myrtano.—*'Tis therefore in Solitude alone I can have Peace;—remov'd from the tumultuous World, its short liv'd Pleasures, and its lasting Cares, I'll languish out a dull, insipid, tranquil Life, and sink by unperceiv'd Degrees into the Grave. And have you no Reluctance,* (resum'd he,) *no soft Regret for all the racking Griefs your noble Father's Heart endures, while ignorant where you are? 'Twas my Design,* (answer'd she,) *to have writ to him from* Verona; *but as I am disappointed of the Journey I intended thither, I have not now Conveniency. If that* (cry'd he, in a Tone which express'd a Zealousness to serve her) *will be anyway conducive to your Satisfaction, I offer myself to be the Messenger.—Prepare a Letter, and it shall be faithfully deliver'd; and whatever other Trust you would repose in me, depend on the Execution of with the same Assurance as tho' you saw it done.*

The prodigious Obligations *Idalia* had receiv'd from him, made her scrupulous of adding to the Number, by giving him any future Troubles; which he perceiving, protested that the highest Recompence she could make for what he had done, was to permit him to continue to do her all the good Offices in his Power: But she, whose Disposition was utterly averse to receiving Favours, especially at a Time when she consider'd herself not in a Condition to return them, would very feign have declin'd making any farther Use of him, telling him she would stay at that House but till she was a little recover'd from the Fatigue she had been in, and then either pursue her Journey to *Verona*, or go to someother Place where there was a Monastery, being absolutely determin'd to become a Nun. But this last Resolution seem'd to alarm him much more than everything she had said before:—And after a little Pause, he let her know that this was not the Way to recompence the Civilities he had done her.—*If you look on anything that I have done* (said he) *as an Obligation, you would permit me to receive my Thanks from Don* Bernardo; *perhaps it may be in his Power to make me ample Reparation for that little Loss of Time 'twill take me up to go to* Venice.—

This Expression, and some others to the same purpose, won her to do as he desire: She consented to write, because her Father should requite the Obligations she had received: But when she was about to do it, never was she at such a Loss in what Manner she should begin, or whether she should conceal or discover the Misfortunes she had met with. At last, after many blottings-out, and tearing, she made a shift to write these few Lines.

### To Don BERNARDO

I Doubt not, most Honoured Seignor, but at the Receipt
of this, you will expect to be satisfied at full, of the Reasons
which have depriv'd you of a Daughter; but it is not the least
of my Misfortunes that they are of such a Nature, that the
disclosing them would add to their Severity.—Pardon then, I
beseech you, that I conceal them even from you,—and with
the same Indulgence I have formerly found, continue to
think of me.—I never can be happy enough to see you more,
being determin'd to forsake the World. As to my Choice
of a Monastery, and what Order I should take, I leave to
your Management, as I shall some Part of my History to
be related to you by the Bearer of this, to whom I not only
indebted for my Life, but also this Opportunity of entreating
your Blessing, and avowing myself ever

Your most Obedient,
tho' Unhappy Daughter,
IDALIA

P.S. My Deliverer informs me it is in Don *Bernardo's* Power
to more than recompence the Obligations he has heap'd
upon *Idalia:*—If so, I know he need no more than to acquaint
you in what Manner to engage your grateful Assent.

With this Letter, she gave to him that was to carry it a Ring from her Finger, entreating him to accept it as an Acknowledgement of her Gratitude, which he received with an Extacy of Joy, a Transport impossible to be conceal'd, and far above what the intrinsick Value of it, meerly as a Ring (had it been worth a thousand Times more that it was) could have raised in the most covetous Mind. She observ'd it with a

Surprise as visible to *him*, as was the Rapture he had been in to *her*; and unwilling she should infer any further from it than he thought proper to declare, *I am extremely glad, Madam*, said he, *of this Testimony, which, to those who employed me, will appear an infallible one, that I have murdered you; and by that Means, perhaps, engage an Addition to the Reward I have already receiv'd.* These last Words were utter'd so awkwardly, and were so little of a Piece with the rest of his Behaviour, that it rather increas'd than diminish'd the Consternation she was in. There pass'd not much more between them; he seem'd in haste to be gone, and only recommending her to the Care of the People of the House, and assuring her, that in a very few Days he would return with an Answer to her Letter, too his Leave.

The Emotions she was in, when left at Liberty to consider on what had befallen her since she came from *Vicenza*, were at once pleasing and vexatious: Her Deliverance from so imminent a Danger, commanded her most thankful Acknowledgments; but then the Confirmation of the Falshood of *Myrtano* made her almost wish for Death:—To reflect on the Behaviour of this unknown Person, led her into such a mazy Labyrinth of Thought, that she could neither get out, nor in the least assure herself where it would end.—There appeared something so contradictory in his Words and Actions, that it was impossible for her to form any Judgment of him.—His Garb was the meanest that could be; but yet there was an undescribable Somewhat in his Air, which spoke him accustomed to wear better.—The Reward he told her he had receiv'd to murder her, would have made her believe he must be of the lowest Rank of Life; but then the noble Detestation which sparkled in his Eyes at mentioning it, declar'd him far above even pretending to enter into such Measures, without some Reason for it, which, at present, she could not penetrate into:—But the most shocking Consideration of all was, that she saw, by his Manner of receiving the Ring,—by some unguarded Words and Sighs, which, in spite of the Care he took to suppress them, burst with Vehemence from his troubled Breast, that her Beauty had had the same Effects on him, it was ordinary for it to cause in others; and as vain and proud of giving Pain, as she had ever been, could not look on this Conquest without the utmost Disquiet: If he was of that inferior Degree he spoke himself, nothing could be more galling than the Thoughts of being belov'd by such a one; and if he were a Man of that Quality, which some Part of his Behaviour denoted, she had Reason enough to fear she had fled from *Vicenza* for no other End than to give an Opportunity to *one* to act what she had done a Violence on her own Inclination to avoid from *another. How wretched is my Fate!* (said she to herself.) *Have I, to preserve my Honour free from any second Stain, broke thro' the soft Enchantments of my Passion, and tore my very Heart-Strings, when I resolved to quit the dear, the lov'd* Myrtano's *House; and am now in the Power of a Stranger, one who looks on me with the same Desires,—the same wild Vehemence of Longing!—One, who, for ought I know, has brought me hither only to do what* Ferdinand *has done, and what* Myrtano *would!*—the more she deliberated, the more she found the Probability of this Conjecture, and, at last, confirm'd herself in the Reality of it so much, that she grew the most terrified Creature that ever was.

More Days had pass'd since the Departure of the Stranger than she expected he would be absent; in which Time she had used her utmost Endeavour to discover who he was, by the old Man and Woman of the House; but they, faithful to the Trust repos'd in them, would not reveal the least Tittle, either of his Name or Family; and his Secrecy did not a little contribute to fix her in that Opinion she before had entertain'd, That she was placed there in order to be the Sacrifice to his Passion as soon as he should return; and put her on a thousand Inventions how to avoid it: But, alas! what would the most subtle working Wit, back'd by the firmest Resolution, avail in a Circumstance such as hers? She was in a Place which she neither knew the Name of, nor in what Part of the Country it stood, and under the Care of People, who she easily perceiv'd, tho' they waited on her with all possible Obedience, had a strict Eye on her Behaviour: For saying to them one Day, with an Intention of sounding them, that if she had a Conveniency, she would go to *Verona* and wait there till either the Stranger should return, or she should hear from her Father by someother Way; they told her they could not consent she should leave them, till they had Permission from the Person who had brought her there. This was sufficient to make her know there was no Possibility of escaping by their Means; but being fully bent some Way or other to do it, she never left racking her Brains, till she had found a Stratagem; which, tho' she could not promise herself she should succeed in, would be of no Prejudice to her if it should fail. She told her old Landlord, that finding herself a little indispos'd, she believ'd it would be of no infinite Service to her Health if she walk'd out in a Morning and Evening to take the Air, as she observ'd he did: *But*, said she, *I do not care to venture in the Dress I have been us'd to*

ELIZA HAYWOOD

appear in, left any Passengers happening to travel this Way, should discover me: It would therefore be the greatest Obligation you could confer on me, if you would provide me with a Habit, whereby I might be disguis'd, and by that Means have the Freedom of ranging thro' those delightful Groves and Meadows, the Prospect of which appears so tempting from my Windows. The old *Trustee* look'd on his Wife all the Time *Idalia* had been speaking, as tho' it was from her Approbation he was to form his Answer; who, as soon as she perceiv'd the other had concluded what she had to say, gave it in this Manner: *I do not think*, (said she) *that our Friend would thank us, if we should deny a Request so far from unreasonable.—The Air, indeed may do the Lady good, and the whimsical Merriment of Men, who, at this Time of Year, come in great Numbers to gather Mulberry-Leaves for their Silk-Worms, divert her Melancholy:—I would have you, by all Means, provide her with a Dress such as our Country Maids are used to wear, and she may pass, and partake of all our rural Pleasures the Time she stays here, without any Danger of Suspicion.* The Heart of *Idalia* leap'd in her Breast at this ready Assent of the Woman's, which was immediately follow'd by her Husband's; and in a few Hours this *Court Beauty* was transform'd into a plain *Country Lass*; and though no Dress could render her any other than the most lovely Woman in the World, yet so great was her Desire to be taken for what she represented, that she mimick'd the Simplicity of their Blushes, and Way of Curts'ying so artfully, that those who were most acquainted with her might have talk'd to her sometime before they discover'd the Deceit.

Having carry'd on her Plot thus far, the next Thing she had to do, was to counterfeit a Chearfulness, and appear so highly satisfy'd with her Condition, that her *Guardians* might not imagine she had any Wishes to exchange it, and be less watchful over her; for wherever she went, they had continually attended her. But her Artifice deceiv'd them so well, that by degrees they grew more remiss, and at length would leave her to the Privilege of meditating, as sometimes she took a Book out with her, or diverting herself with talking or listening to the comical Discourses of the Country Fellows employ'd in tying the Vines, and gathering Mulberry-Leaves. She would not take her Flight the first Opportunity she had, because she did not know but they might have left her only to make trial what she would do, and be near enough to prevent her going, in case she should attempt it: But one Day, having neither of them within hearing, she enquir'd, as tho' without Design, what Towns were in the Neighbourhood of that Place; and was inform'd, that she was about forty Miles from any, but that the nearest was *Vorseny*. It was no small Grief to her to hear she was so remote, not believing she could be able to travel so far on Foot: However, nothing being so dreadful to her as the Apprehensions what might befal her, if she tarry'd where she was, she resolv'd to run all other Hazards to escape that; and looking on it as a particular Mark of the Care Providence had of her, in delaying the Stranger's Return so much longer than was expected, she thought it would be no other than running wilfully into a Misfortune, to neglect making use of the smallest Means that should offer to take her from it. The very next Time therefore that she found herself free from Observation of her two Attendants, she walk'd as fast as her Strength would permit, directed by the Sun, thro' that Part of the Country which she had been told led her to *Vorseny*. She came at length to a great Road, where she saw Numbers of poor People of both Sexes driving Asses before them, loaded with these Leaves, which they had gather'd in the Morning, and were carrying to the Merchants. It was no small Consolation to the fair Wanderer to have something of her own Species to converse with, having till now met with no other Company in her Pilgrimage than the Dumb Kind.—But being ask'd by some of them, whither she was going, and how it happen'd that such a fair young Maid undertook so great a Journey alone, and on Foot, she was at the greatest Loss in the World what Answer to make; till at last, bethinking herself what would be most suitable to the Capacities of those who enquir'd, and best disguise the Truth, she told them, That having a very severe Mother-in-Law, she had fled from her ill Usage, and was going to seek a Service at *Vorseny*. The good People pity'd her extremely; and perceiving she was ready to faint with Weariness, contriv'd a Way to set her on one of their Beasts, by taking off its Burden of Leaves, and dividing it into as many Parcels as there were Asses, added a little to everyone. By this Means she got safe to the Town; and thanking her Fellow-Travellers for their Kindness, and there took Leave of them. She went into a common Inn, being in no danger of being known in that Place, especially in the Garb she was in. The Fatigue she had undergone, made it necessary she should for sometime repose herself: But, alas! the Disorders of her Mind would suffer her to take but little Rest, the various Adventures she had run thro' since that fatal Time of going to meet the perfidious *Florez*, the Grief her Absence and Disgrace had brought on her unhappy *Father*,—the Death of *Henriquez*,—her own eternal Ruin by the Violence of *Ferdinand*,—the Agonies she had, and ever must endure for the Falshood of the lovely *Myrtano*,—the Terror she had been in from the discover'd Passion of the Unknown,—and the racking Perplexity where, or in what manner she should linger out the Residue of her unhappy Days, came all at once into her Thoughts, and threw her into a Condition little different from Madness.

Some Weeks pass'd before she could get leave of her Confusion to resolve on anything, till the little Stock of Money she had about her being pretty near exhausted, she began to consider that this was not a Place to continue in; and remembring that a young Lady, formerly an Intimate of her's, having on some Discontent forsook the World, was at a Convent of *Benedictines* at *Naples*, she promis'd herself a good deal of Satisfaction in her Company, if by any Means she could reach thither: But it was so prodigious a Distance by Land, that it would require infinitely more to defray the Expence of such a Journey, than she was Mistress of. She therefore thought it the best Way to go first to *Ancona*; which being a great Sea-Port Town, she did not doubt meeting with a Vessel there bound for the Place she desir'd. Everything answer'd her Expectations; and nothing of any Moment happening till she was got on Board, I shall omit the Repetition of any Particulars of her little Journey, or the Uneasiness she was in while she staid at *Ancona*, which she was oblig'd to do, the Ship she had agreed to go in not being ready to fail in above a Month, and when it was, detain'd almost as long by adverse Winds.

The Power of Beauty is the same in all Degrees; the plain Country Habit which disguis'd the Daughter of a *Grandee*, could not deprive *Idalia* of her wonted Charms: She appear'd so lovely in the Eyes of *Rickamboll*, the Captain of the Ship, that from the first Moment he beheld her, he thought of nothing but the Means to posses her. He conceal'd his Intentions, however, till she was come on Board; but he no sooner had her in his Power, than he let her know he would make use of it for the Gratification of his Passion, if she consented not to yield to his Perswasions.

What was now the Anguish, the Fear, the Horror, which seiz'd the Soul of this unhappy Lady? All that was pass'd appear'd a Blessing to her present State; confin'd within a little wooden World, whose proud Sovereign was absolute, and from the Fierceness of whose Nature she had no room to hope that Prayers or Tears would be of Force to melt him!—Here was no Possibility of escaping but by immediate Death; and what she suffer'd in the Apprehension of his Brutality, is not to be described by Words; so I shall only say, it was such as could be equalled by nothing but his barbarous Insensibility of it. Trembling, fainting, and almost dying with her Fears, she was on her Knees in her Cabin imploring Heaven's Protection, when the Monster, resolved to perpetrate his horrid Wishes, came in to know her last Resolve. Perceiving his Intent, she would fain have flatter'd him into a Belief there was a Possibility of gaining her by gentle Means, and entreated him but to have Patience till they came on Shore: But he, who understood no more of Love than the brutal Part, burning to enjoy her, and not suspecting her to be of any higher Station than what her Habit represented, thought to make use of any further Ceremony would be an Indignity to himself, and by his *Actions*, as well as *Words*, let her see he was not to be moved. In vain she endeavour'd to set forth the Baseness of the Deed;—in vain she wept, entreated, threaten'd; the Villain harden'd in such Crimes, but laugh'd at her Despair, and she was just on the Point of being reduced to a Condition, such as, if she had lived after it, would have made her forever hateful to herself, when Heaven, by the most unexpected Means, sent her a Deliverance. The Oaths and Curses, with which the boisterous *Rickamboll* had endeavour'd to Silence her Shrieks, on a sudden were out-done by a confused and superior Roar on Deck; and immediately after a Discharge of Guns went off so loud, the Ship seem'd shatter'd with Noise!—A General Voice cry'd, *Where's our Captain?* and three or four of the affrighted Sailors burst into the Cabin, bawling out in their rude Fashion, That they were undone; a *Barbary Corsair* had clapp'd his grappling Irons on Board, and Death or Captivity was all they could expect.—*'s Death! could you not avoid him? Had you no Warning?* said *Rickamboll*, starting from his amorous Combat: *But he shall find no Cowards here*. With these Words he run out of the Cabin, follow'd by the rest of the Men, leaving the distress'd *Idalia* in a Dilemma, to which Party she should with Success. If *Rickamboll* was victorious, she had no hope of escaping the Ill his wild Desires threaten'd her with, and Slavery itself seem'd far less dreadful to her:—But then the Thoughts of being in the Power of *Infidels*, who, 'twas highly probable, might be inspired with the same Wishes, and would make no Scruple to use a *Christian Captive* as they pleased, frighted her almost to Death.—The Apprehensions of what she expected would ensue, whatever was the Issue of the Fight, drown'd all the Terrors of the *present* Danger, which, whoever has been Witness of one of these Sea-Skirmishes, may easily comprehend: But it lasted not long, the Number of the *Infidels* was infinitely superior to the *Christians*, and by the Death of *Rickamboll*, and some of the stoutest of his Men, the rest of them, with the Ship, became an easy Prize. *Idalia*, all this while at her Devotions, was ignorant of what had happen'd, till she saw a Stranger of a most graceful Mein, attended by several Followers, come down the Stairs, and enter the *Cabin* where she was. *Abdomar* (for that was the Name of this Conquerer) had been formerly a Prisoner at *Florence*, and spoke very good *Italian*; which was no inconsiderable Piece of good Fortune to this *fair Captive*, for the obliging Terms he accosted her with (in spite of the Meanness of her Habit) dissipated, immediately, great part of her Fears; and reading in her Tears and Tremblings the Agony she was in, *Be of Comfort, lovely Maid*, said he, *you are fallen into the Power of one, who scorns to take an ungenerous Advantage of it,—one who has it not in his Nature willingly to offend any of your Sex, much less one to whom Heaven has been so particularly bountiful in bestowing all that can command Respect.—Your Lot, perhaps,* (continued he, perceiving she was still in some Disorder) *may become more glorious by this Captivity, than Freedom could offer you the Means to make it;—the most angelick, softest, kindest, best that ever was call'd Woman, will by her Tenderness and Indulgence, make you forget whatever may have been dear to you, and oblige you to place your whole Felicity, as it will be your Honour to be near her.*—Nothing in *Idalia's* present Circumstance could have afforded her a Consolation adequate to these last Words: To hear he was a Lover, and that he was accompanied by his Adored, entirely set her free from those Apprehensions which of late had been so afflicting to her. And as soon as he had given Orders for securing the other Prisoners under Hatches, suffer'd herself to be conducted by him into that Ship of which he was Commander, with all the Chearfulness imaginable; as thinking, in being deliver'd from the brutal Attempt of *Rickamboll*, she had been deliver'd from the most terrible Misery that could befall her. *Abdomar* led her immediately into a Cabin, adorn'd with the choicest Curiosities which Art could produce in all the various Climates of the habitable World; the Floor was cover'd with the most rich, as well as most beautiful Tapestry that ever was seen; the Ground was Silver, on which were so dextrously interwoven all manner of fine Flowers, that they seem'd more the Handy-work of Nature than of human Skill; the Windows, which *without* were fenced from the dashing of the Waves with Crystal in the manner of half Globes, *within* were chequer'd with green and gold Twist, each square being join'd with precious Stones: Diamonds, Rubies, Emeralds, Chrysolites, and Saphirs, with their various colour'd Lustre, spread such a dazzling Glory round the Room, that it even pain'd the Eye to look upon it: The greatest Magnificence that ever *Idalia* had beheld in *Venice*, than which no City in the World can boast of more, was so infinitely short of what now met her Eyes, that she had longer and more heedfully regarded it, had not a greater, and yet surpassing Wonder appear'd to attract her Admiration; it was the charming *Bellraizia*, Mistress of *Abdomar*, who, rising from a Couch of Crimson Taffety embroider'd with Gold and Pearl, stepp'd forward to meet and congratulate her Lover on his Victory. She spoke to him in the Language of their own Country, but there was something so sweet, so soft, so engaging in her Voice, that render'd it an Impossibility to hear her, without feeling some Part of that Pleasure which the looking on her did in a greater abundance bestow. To the most lovely and enchanting Form that Nature ever made, there was also added all the Embelishments of Art:—Had she been in a Court where it was the sole Business of all about her to study what would most become her, she cou'd not have been dress'd with greater Elegance: Her Hair, which was whiter, and more shining than Silver, and hung down in Tresses below her Waste, was only kept from falling o'er her Face by a Fillet of Diamonds; but as the greatest *Art* is to appear *artless*, this seeming Negligence had in it something so infinitely beyond the formal Ornaments of the *Europeans*, that whoever would desire to please, must covet to look like this lovely *Barbarian*. On the Middle of the Fillet there was fix'd a sort of a little Tree of Gold, on the Branches of which hung Jewels of a prodigious Largeness, but such a Height above her Head, that (the Sprigs on which they were fasten'd being shaded by some loose Hair, which flew out as tho' disdainful of Restraint) made it seem to the Eye as tho' they were self-poiz'd, and form'd a Constellation like *Araidne's* Crown. On her slender and fine proportion'd Body, she had a close Jacket of Gold Stuff; but the Sleeves were large, and tied up before almost as high as her Shoulders, with small Sky-coloured Ribband mixed with Silver, and discover'd, as much as Decency would permit, her lovely Arms, which were encompass'd with Bracelets of several sorts of Jewels. In fine, her whole Appearance, her Face, her Shape, her Hair, her Habit, was surpassing what the most extensive Imagination can figure out, and forc'd *Idalia* (who was not over quick-sighted to the Perfections of her own Sex) whether she would or no, to

ELIZA HAYWOOD

confess within herself, that she had never seen anything so beautiful! so glorious!

After some little Discourse between the two Lovers, *Abdomar* presenting *Idalia*, said in *Italian, What other Prizes my late Conquest has made me Master of, I thought unworthy of* Bellraizia's *Notice; but this fair Maid, if she appear the same in your Eyes, as at first Sight she did to mine, may merit to attend you.* The charming *Infidel* answered these Words in Terms infinitely obliging to *Idalia*; but afterwards enquiring her Name, Family, whither she had designed to go, and for what Reason so young a Maid had undertaken a Voyage, unaccompanied by any Friends or Relations, and other Particulars of her Life, the new-made *Slave* could make no other Reply than with her Tears; which the other perceiving, and knowing well by Experience to what Extreams Love can transport the Heart that owns his Power, and imagining by her Mein, and something of a grand Look about her, which no Disguise could rob her of, that she was of a Quality superior to what she was willing to confess, would press her no farther at that Time; but desiring her to be as easy with her Fate as possible, and assuring her she should find nothing of Severity in her Servitude, commanded some of her other *Slaves* to place her in a Cabin, and leave her to that Repose which, 'twas probable, after the late Fright the Danger of the Fight had put her in, she might stand need of.

In spite of the various Reflections this unhappy *Fair* had on this sudden and prodigious Alteration of her own Affairs, she could not forbear forgetting them a while, to contemplate on those of the Lady whom she must now call *Mistress*. It appeared so odd that a Woman, such as the Looks and Habit of *Bellraizia* spoke her to be, should be the willing Partaker of Dangers, Fatigues, and Horrors, such as were inseparable from the Profession of *Abdomar*, that she could not but think there was something very extraordinary in the Adventure: But her Surprise was very much heighten'd, when the next Morning she was summon'd with the rest of the Slaves (who at several Times had been taken by *Abdomar*) to rise and attend the *Princess*; and she could not forbear asking the Person who brought her this Command some Questions concerning this Affair, but could learn no more from him, than that *Bellraizia* was of the Royal Blood of *Barbary*; and that for the Love of *Abdomar*, who was also of a high Extraction, tho' banish'd for some Misdemeanor, she had forsook her Country, and chose to love a Rover on that uncertain Element, despising all the Dangers of it for his sake. This Information threw the poor *Idalia* into Anxieties much worse than her Captivity had inflicted on her;—the Passion she had for *Myrtano*, which her late Frights had silenced for a while, now rouz'd itself within her Soul, and told her how happy might she have been, had he been true;—how joyfully she could have embraced *Bellraizia's* Fate, had *Myrtano*, like *Abdomar*, been just. *Oh! had that lovely Youth* (cry'd she to herself) *returned my Passion with an equal Ardour, what is it I would not have endured?—what Dangers could I not have dar'd?—what Sufferings could I not with Joy have born to keep him mine? Pain would have been unfelt, Want lost its Sting, and even Death a Blessing for his sake!—My humble Wishes aspired no higher than to be wretched with* Myrtano,—*yet that the cruel Heavens deny!—Miserable* Idalia! *where,—where will thy Sorrows end!* The violent Agitations of her Soul oppress'd her here so strongly, that unable to repel their Force, she fell in the Bed she was sitting on entirely motionless; nor recovered she, till being a second time sent for by *Bellraizia*, and found in that Condition, all Means that could be invented were made use of for her Relief; and so extremely concerned was her generous Conquerer, and his admir'd Mistress, that they both join'd in giving her a thousand Assurances of their Pity, and a Grant of whatever was in either of their Powers, to remedy the Misfortunes she labour'd under: *If it be Captivity alone that makes you wretched,* said *Bellraizia, I dare promise you a Release as well from that Compassion which is natural to the noble* Abdomar, *as from the ready Compliance I have ever found in him to any Request of mine; be therefore comforted, for be assured whatever Pleasure I might take in retaining a Person whose Conversation I think so desirable as yours, I would not for the Universe have my Soul loaded with the Guilt of rendering you unhappy. Idalia* answered these obliging Expressions in Terms full of Gratitude, and Respect; and the other taking an Opportunity of *Abdomar's* being gone out of the Cabin on some Business which called him on Deck, entreated her, if it were not too great a Secret, to relate the Particulars of her Life. This was not a Task so easy to be perform'd as she imagin'd; there were some Passages which were an Offence to her Modesty to *remember*, much more to *repeat*; and others, which the Description of would add to her Affliction, by suffering again in *Idea* what she had before in *Reality*: However, the Obligations she had to *Bellraizia*, and the Impossibility there was of denying anything to a Person who asked with so good a Grace, surmounted all these Scruples, and she recounted to her both who she was, how she had been betray'd from her

Father's House by the Perfidiousness of *Florez*, the Violence that had been offered to her by Don *Ferdinand*, the unhappy Quarrel between him and *Henriquez*, their Deaths, her Passion for *Myrtano*, the Terrors she had endur'd in the Apprehension of a second Violation from him, and afterwards the unknown Person appointed for her Guide, and this last of *Rickamboll*, from which the Victory of *Abdomar* had so fortunately deliver'd her.

This Story, had it been told by any other Person, and stripp'd of all those grief-attracting Illustrations which heightened each unlucky Accident in *Idalia's* Description, was in itself too moving not to excite the tenderest Compassion in the Soul of her who heard it. *Abdomar* at his Return found them both drown'd in Tears; which enquiring the Reason of, *That* (reply'd the Charmer of his Soul) *which when you are acquainted with, will very near bring you into our Condition; your beautiful Prisoner's Misfortunes,—she has been giving me an Account so full of Wonder, that when you hear it, as with her Leave someother Time you shall, I know you will join in my Belief, that Heaven designs her for some extraordinary Event.* The afflicted *Idalia* would have made some Return to these Words, but was too much overcome by her Disorders, and entreated the Liberty of retiring to the Cabin appointed for her. The obliging *Bellraizia* would needs accompany her, and was so assiduous in her Endeavours to asswage her Sorrow, that the other, if in *reality* she found no Consolation, thought herself bound in Gratitude and Complaisance to seem as if she did. As they were talking, she happen'd to let fall some Words which discover'd a Desire of knowing the Adventures of a Lady, whom she esteemed so infinitely happy in the Society of the Man she loved. *'Tis a general Observation* (said she) *that those Things we place our chief Felicity in, are the farthest from our Reach, it being the Sport of adverse Fate, to wound us in the tenderest Part: But you, Madam, and the noble* Abdomar, *are a blest Exception to that Rule, and having all in one another, can know no second Wish.* 'Tis true, replied *Bellraizia, we are at last as happy as Love can make us; but did you know the Toils, the Dangers, the Endurings we have had,—the unintermitting Cares, incessant Fears, and little Hopes, which, in the Race of Passion, both accompany'd, you'd be surpris'd that either of us liv'd to reach the* Goal: *And because I know not but it may alleviate a Despair I see is beginning to take Root in you, to hear that there are no Misfortunes so great but Heaven can relieve us from, I shall, if you desire it, let you into the most secret History of mine.* Idalia immediately told her there was not a Possibility of her conferring a greater Obligation;—that it was a Favour she had been ambitious of since the first Moment she was brought before her; and that having now so favourable an Opportunity of their being alone, begg'd she would make use of it for that Purpose. To which *Bellraizia* willingly complying, began to entertain her with what she desired, in this Manner:

*The History of* Abdomar *and* Bellraizia.

In the Little Time, *said she*, you have been in our Ship, you may, perhaps, have heard of what Country I am a Native, and doubtless are surpris'd to see my Complexion so different from others born in the same Climate; but to ease you of that Wonder, I must let you know the first of my Family that settled in *Barbary* was a Renegade Christian, a *Florentine*, nearly ally'd to the Great Duke of *Tuscany*, and General of his Forces; who, quitting his Service on some Disgust, brought his Family to *Barbary*, renounc'd his Religion, and was promoted. A sudden War breaking out, he signaliz'd himself by many remarkable Actions, and at his Return was made Governor of a Province, in which Post he dy'd. Great Revolutions afterwards happening, a Son of his was advanc'd to the Dignity of *Bassaw*; and in Length of Time, and, to them, an auspicious Turn of Fortune, a Descendant of his to the *Crown*, under an annual Tribute to the Emperor of *Morocco*, my Father's Brother is at present King, and the fifth Monarch of our Race. I make you not this Relation as a Boast of my Pedigree, but as it is necessary, to render other Occurences plain to your Observation; for had my Birth been meaner, my Lot had been more bless'd; Grandeur has only given me an adequate Portion of Inquietudes; and Fate, by placing me in so elevated a State, had no other Design in it, than to make me more remarkably unhappy. My Uncle having but one Daughter, oblig'd my Father to let me be bred with her at Court, for a Companion in all her Diversions; and with our Years there grew so tender a Friendship between us, as is very rarely to be found in Persons of the same Sex: Neither of us had a Desire, tho' never so violent, that we could not resign for the Gratification of the other: If Joy or Sorrow sat on the Face of *either*, you might be certain to find it in the other's also. Thus, bless'd with that Tranquility which is always inseparable to those who are possess'd of Innocence and Freedom, did we live, till *Love!*—that sweet destructive Passion! that luscious Poisoner of the Calm of Life! chang'd that felicitous State for Cares, Inquietudes, and unceasing Perturbations!

The King of *Fez* had a Son esteem'd the Wonder of his Age: His Martial Exploits had justly made him famous over all that Quarter of the World; nor was his soft Address, and elegant Behaviour, less charming to his Friends, than his undaunted Fierceness was dreadful to his Enemies.—I know not what ill Star inclin'd him to make a Visit at our Court; but he had no sooner arriv'd there, and cast his Eyes on me, than he became enamour'd. I, who at that Time had a Heart entirely unprepossess'd, and was not without out some Share of that Vanity by which most of our Sex, more or less, are sway'd, could not listen to the Declarations he made me, without an adequate Proportion of Pride and Pleasure, for being capable of inspiring a Prince so every way agreeable with a Passion such as he profess'd. My Uncle, who truly lov'd me, extremely approv'd of the Proposals he made, and my Father thought himself so much honour'd by them, that he laid the strictest Command on me to treat *Mulyzeden* (for that was his Name) as a Prince, to whose Professions of Love I was infinitely oblig'd. Never was Lover indulg'd, on all Sides, with so many Opportunities of expressing his Passion, yet was he not contented: He was always complaining, that not all the Solicitations he made were effectual to inspire me with Sentiments such as he wish'd:—He tormented himself with a Belief, that the Deference I paid him, was wholly owing to his Quality, and the Commands my Uncle and Father had given me:—He never saw me without telling me he found it impossible to make me love him; but one Day he seem'd so uneasy, and indeed so desperate at my Insensibility, as he call'd it, that I thought he was distracted. For my Part, I believ'd I lov'd him: I had never seen a Man whose Merits I could think equal to those he was master of;—was perfectly pleas'd when in his Company; and on the strictest Examination into my own Heart, could find in it not the least Scruple at becoming his Wife, which Title I had consented to wear, as soon as the necessary Preparations to confer it on me could be got ready.—I did not fail to acquaint him with the most favourable of my Inclinations; but all I could say, was insufficient to give him the Consolation I wish'd:—He still accus'd me of Coldness. Nor indeed is it to be wonder'd at, that he did so: For, alas! he perceiv'd nothing in me of those tender Langours,—those melting Softnesses,—those pleasing Pains,—those thrilling Ardours,—those mingled Hopes and Fears, which still accompany Desire, and are never at an End, till sure Possession cuts them off,—those thousand, thousand, nameless Consequences of eager Passion, which he felt, and could easily distinguish, and which I since have too powerfully experienc'd!—But at that Time, I was utterly ignorant what it was he meant whene'er he nam'd them to me, and began to think him unreasonable to ask greater Proofs of my Affection, than what I imagin'd was in the Power of any Woman to give.— Perceiving I grew angry at these kind of Discourses, he at length forbore them; but in doing so, put so great a Constraint on his Inclinations, as, could I have had any Notion of what I now am certain he suffer'd, would have made me endure almost as much thro' *Pity*, as he did from an Agitation more violent. But not to tire you with the Particulars of our Behaviour till the Day appointed for the Celebration of our Nuptials was arriv'd, which had not been so long delay'd, but for the expected coming of a young Nobleman of *Fez*, one who from his Infancy had been brought up with *Mulyzeden*, as I had with the Princess of my Cousin, and so firmly united were they in Friendship, that fearing *Marriage* might sometime or other occasion a *Slack'ning*, if not a total *Breach* of that Bond which both desir'd should be *indissoluble*, each had taken an Oath never to wed, but with the Approbation of the other. *Mulyzeden* had so sacred a Regard to his Promise in this Affair, that as soon as he had obtain'd mine and my Parent's Consent to make me his, he dispatch'd a Messenger to *Fez* with an Account of the Progress he had made, and entreating the Presence of this dear *Favourite*. The other was not neglectful of the Duty he ow'd to his Prince and Friend, but set out for *Barbary* the Moment he was recover'd of some slight Wounds, which had been the Cause of his staying behind him, as to avoid marrying a Lady whom his Father had provided for him, was of *Mulyzeden's* coming away. It was Evening when he came to *Court*, and being engag'd with the Princess, I saw him not that Night. I had observ'd an unusual Melancholy in that young Princess; but she complaining of a little Indisposition in her Head, made me impute it to that, and prevented my taking so much Notice of it, as otherwise I should have done; but the News of the Prince's Favourite's Arrival being blaz'd about the Court, she sent for me immediately. I found her on the Bed in such Agony of Grief, that I should but lessen it in an Endeavour to represent it.—It was a good while before she was able to speak to me, tho' she attempted it several Times, and it was with the utmost Difficulty she at last brought out these Words:—*Pity me! pity me,* Bellraizia!—*Dearest Cousin, pity me!*—She would have proceeded, but the struggling Passions of her Soul stopp'd her Utterance, and Sighs, accompany'd with a Torrent of Tears, had alone the Power of informing me she labour'd under some very great Affliction. The Surprise I was in to see her in this Manner, did not hinder me from endeavouring to console her; but when I entreated her to reveal what 'twas disturb'd her, she seem'd possess'd with an Addition of Disquiet. *Press me no more,* (said she, with a Countenance which, without the Help of Words, sufficiently express'd the Distress of her Soul,) *the Misfortune I am fallen under, nor Earth, nor Heaven can relieve me from:—Why then should I afflict you with the Knowledge of it?* The Accent in which she spoke this, touch'd me to the Heart: I tenderly lov'd her, and could not bear to see her thus, and be ignorant of the Cause: I fell on my Knees by the Bedside, and kissing her Hand, and bathing it in my Tears, which now fell fast as her's, conjur'd her by all the Friendship she had favour'd me with, to let me into the cruel Secret of her Sorrows.—*I cannot,—must not,—dare not tell you,* answer'd she. *O Heavens!* interrupted I, *what can have happen'd to* Zatilda, (for that was her Name,) *that* Bellraizia *must not know! Nay,* (continu'd I,) *I think you said you dare not speak it;—and I have just Cause to fear you doubt my Truth, if longer you refuse to give me leave to join with you in your Complainings. No, no,* (resum'd she, hastily,) *you have no Cause to mourn.—Fate is about to give you all you can desire; therefore I'll not detain you from the dear Presence of the Prince who adores you, and whom justly you esteem;—I sent for you, but to take my last Farewell, for be assur'd I'll not out-live this Night: No,* (pursu'd she, raising her Eyes to Heaven, as tho' she meant to accuse the Gods for her Misfortunes,) *no, I ne'er will live to see Tomorrow's hated Dawn,—this Night shall put an End to curs'd* Zatilda's *Misery and Shame.* It would be impossible for me to express either my Confusion at the first Part of her Discourse, or the Agonies I felt at the Resolution which she clos'd it with:—The sudden Tremblings which seiz'd her, and the visible Alteration in her Countenance when she nam'd the *Prince*; gave me some little faint *Idea*, that it was he who had been so fatal to her Repose, and in so surprising a Juncture was not Mistress of Presence enough of Mind to be able to resolve in what Manner I should reply.— While I was pausing, she had been endeavouring to recollect herself; and perhaps believing she had said too much, was willing to break off any farther Conversation,—*I see,* cry'd she, *I see (with an Infinity of Concern for having occasion'd it) how nearly the Despair you find me in has touch'd you. Pardon it, I beseech you, my dear* Bellraizia! *'tis the last Trouble you will ever receive from the unfortunate* Zatilda:—*Remember me, I conjure you,* (added she, tenderly pressing my Hand;) *and when you are possess'd of all your Soul is fond of in* Mulyzeden's *Court, think he cannot love you more than I have done!*—And then, (perceiving I was silent, for indeed I had not yet the Power of Speech, so much had Amazement lock'd up all my Senses,) Go, (continu'd she,) *I will no longer afflict you with the Sight of Woe, it is not in your Power to remedy: Go, go, and be bless'd with* Mulyzeden! The Hesitation with which she still pronounc'd that Name, confirm'd me that my Conjectures had but too real a Foundation; and at last getting leave from the Whirl of Thought which that Belief had at the first involv'd me in, *It is not in Nature*, (answer'd I,) *for* Bellraizia *to know what Felicity is, when* Zatilda *refuses to be Partaker of it; that* Prince *you speak of, deserving as he is, had never the Power to rival you in my Affections;—nor shall my Uncle, my Father, his ardent Passion, or my own, oblige me to become his Wife, if you approve not of it.* She would by some faint Arguments have perswaded me to believe, there was nothing she more desir'd than to see me Princess of *Fez*; but she was so little accustom'd to Hypocrisy, that I easily distinguish'd her *Heart* was far from assenting to what her *Tongue* had utter'd, and that all the Pains she took, was but to disguise a Truth her Modesty could not suffer her to wish disclos'd. But I, who was not able to bear to *see*, much less to *leave* her in this Anxiety, press'd her so home, that at length I wrested the Secret from her Breast, and found it as I imagin'd. I had several Messages from *Mulyzeden*, while I was employ'd in comforting her, to let me know, That this long-expected Friend was now arriv'd, and that they both waited at my Apartment; but I still sent Excuses, and at last a plain Denial, that I would not be seen that Night. The *King* being told of his Daughter's Indisposition, came also into her Chamber; and seeing me there, told me the Prince of *Fez* depended on the Performance of my Promise of marrying him the next Day. To which I answer'd, That with his Majesty's Permission, I would defer it till the Princess *Zatilda* should be enough recover'd to be Witness of the Ceremony. He seem'd oblig'd to the Concern I express'd for her, and told me, That if my Father and the Prince would be so content, he would not oppose what I desir'd. *Zatilda* look'd on me while I was speaking in this Manner to her Father, with a Mixture of Astonishment and Joy, but durst not express any Part of what she thought before him, lest the Secret should be as liable to his Suspicion, as she knew it had been to mine: But the Moment he had left the Room, demanded of me impatiently what it was I meant, by requesting to delay the Marriage. *I mean*, said I, *by protracting, to shift it off entirely.—How!* (cry'd she, with a Voice which express'd the highest Transport,) *is it then possible you do not love him? Not half enough to make you unhappy,* (reply'd I.) To repeat the thousand Acknowledgments, the Kisses, the Embraces, she gave me at this Declaration, would but tire you; it shall suffice to say the Night was taken up with them, and the Study what Means should be made use of to disappoint *Mulyzeden* of his Hopes of me, and turn the Course of his Affections where they were with more Zeal desir'd. We had a thousand Inventions, but none seemed plausible enough to be approv'd, and the enamour'd Princess was oblig'd to content herself with the repeated Assurances, that neither Force nor Entreaty should prevail on me to make her miserable by my yielding to be his Wife, and leave to Time and Chance to work for her, in changing the Sentiments he had for me to her Advantage.

When Morning came, I left her in a much better Condition of Repose than that in which I had found her, and retired to my own Appartment not a little satisfy'd to have an Opportunity of reflecting on what I had done. The Advantage I propos'd to myself in being the Wife of a Prince so accomplish'd as *Mulyzeden*, was too great for me to think of quitting without some Concern, and the Promise which my Love to *Zatilda* had oblig'd me to make her of doing so, I foresaw would be very difficult for me to make good: I very well knew, that my Father would fly into the utmost Extremity of Rage against me, when once he should find an Intention in me to oppose his Inclinations. Besides, I could not help having some little Commiseration for a *Prince* who lov'd me with so high a Degree of Passion, that the Loss of me might probably deprive him of his Life. As I was revolving on this Manner, my Page brought me Word he waited for Admittance: I was sensible he must have heard of the Petition I had made the King the Night before, for delaying the Nuptials till *Zatilda's* Recovery, and expected he would reproach the little Regard I shew'd for him, with as much Vehemence as his Respect would give him Leave, but as *that* would be the most plausible, nay, indeed, the *only* Pretence I could make, I resolv'd to have Recourse to no other. I found I was not mistaken: The Moment he enter'd the Room, I read in his Eyes the Discontent of his Soul; and tho' he approach'd me with the most perfect Humility, yet there was something in his Air which told me, before he spoke, that he thought himself ill treated. I had little to say in Vindication of what I had done, since if I had really been possess'd of that Warmth of Passion he had endeavour'd inspire, and which I had often feign'd to make him easy, no Consideration would have been of force to have engag'd me to break the Promise I had made of being his, the very Moment that his

Friend was arrived. Besides, the *Princess's* Indisposition was look'd upon so slight, that (as Lovers are always industrious to torment themselves) he imagin'd it was by my Desire she only counterfeited it, on purpose to give me and Excuse for delaying what I had no Inclination to perform. He express'd himself on this Head in Terms so moving, and complain'd of my Indifference, and the cruel Pleasure I took in making him unhappy, that tho' I was farther from a Passion for him, than, till I knew what it was to *love* in Reality, I was sensible of myself, yet I had a Softness in my Soul which gave me Agonies inexpressible, for being oblig'd by a so severe a Necessity to reduce him to such Despair: But to palliate the Matter as well as I could, I told him, As he was not ignorant of the Friendship which was between my *Cousin* and myself, he ought not to wonder I deny'd to receive what Fortune's Smiles would bestow on me, while she was unable to taste any Joy;—I assur'd him she was in a much worse Condition than was generally believ'd; and finding nothing else would be of force to perswade him to Moderation, was oblig'd to renew the Vows I had before made him, of being his forever, as soon as she was restor'd to her former Health. Unhappy *Prince*! he little suspected the Equivocation of these Words, which when I spoke I knew wou'd be but little to his Advantage; for I resolved she should continue to feign herself as she was, till something should happen to give a Turn to this Affair. He appear'd a little more satisfy'd than he had been, however; and when he was so, told me, the young Nobleman being now arriv'd, attended my Permission to kiss my Hands. I, who had as much Curiosity to see a Person I had heard so much of, as the Chagrin I was in would allow room for, desir'd he might be immediately introduc'd:—But, O Gods! with what Emotions did my Bosom swell when first I cast my Eyes upon him!—I will not go about to represent what 'twas I felt,—'twould be impossible!—But you, lovely *Idalia*! who have so much experienc'd what Passion is, may guess.—Besides, in my fond Judgment, whoever has seen the graceful Form of *Abdomar*, for it was no other, cannot he surpris'd to hear the Effect it wrought on me. How mean, me thought, did *Mulyzeden* seem! how little in comparison with his charming Friend! The Disorder I had been in, while talking to the Prince, serv'd to screen that additional one which seiz'd me at the Sight of the adorable Stranger, from the Observation of them both; for the former took it for no other than what was occasion'd by Reflection on what had been said to me; and the latter, as he has since told me, for a Look that was natural to me: He found enough in it, however, to think agreeable; and 'tis certain, that at this first View, the God of soft Desires fix'd his Arrows in both our Hearts at once: But, alas! I was not so happy to imagine I had made any Impression on him, and *Love* was scarce a Moment older than *Despair*.—It was now that I began to pity poor *Zatilda's* Case, for having entertain'd a Passion for a *Prince*, who seem'd so little in a Capacity of returning it, much more than was in my Power to do before I felt the same. It is not to be express'd, it is not to be imagin'd, what I endur'd while they were present; but (much for my Ease, who long'd for an Opportunity of indulging the new Sentiments I was possess'd with) they stay'd not long, perhaps thinking a Morning Visit might be troublesome, especially to a Person who, that they might do so, had inform'd them she took but little Repose the Night before. But, Oh! how little do they know their Passion's Force, who think to conquer it, by reflecting on the Difficulties that are likely to oppose it!—All that might be inflicted on me from the Indignation of my Royal Uncle, my Father, or the just Resentment of the injur'd *Mulyzeden*, seem'd light to me, if by my Sufferings I cou'd purchase the least Share in his Affections, who was now dearer to me than the whole World besides.—But the most, and indeed the *only* dreadful Consideration was, That should he ever guess at the Inclinations I had for him, he would be so far from thinking himself obliged to them, that he would rather hate me for the Ingratitude I was guilty of to a *Prince* he so infinitely loved. I thought myself now in a much worse Condition than *Zatilda* was, because I had not only the Weight of my own Troubles to support, but was also loaded with those my ill Fate oblig'd me to inflict on *Mulyzeden*, whom, tho' it was not my Destiny to *love*, I could not but have a very tender Regard for. And sure, never was a Soul so torn as mine: I saw the two Persons, for whom I had the greatest Friendship, about to be reduced to the last Degree of Misery on my Account; the one because I did not love him, and the other because I was beloved; while I myself vainly struggled with the Violence of a Passion which I had then no more Hopes of being successful in, than I had of being able to overcome it. Confus'd and wild with these different Agitations, my Brain grew giddy, and Apprehension such a Torment, that I cou'd no longer bear it: I flew to *Zatilda's* Appartment, and found some little Ease in pouring out my Discontents on the Bosom of that faithful Friend. She, who besides the Kindness she ever had for me, thought herself so infinitely oblig'd to me, for the Promise I had made of resigning my Right in *Mulyzeden* to her, did all she cou'd to give me

Consolation; but tho' she truly commiserated my unhappy State, yet I cou'd easily perceive she was not so much dissatisfy'd, as she pretended, at the Relation I made her how much I was influenc'd by the Charms of *Abdomar*. Nor indeed was it natural to believe she shou'd, since this new Passion was a more convincing Assurance that I would never be the Wife of *Mulyzeden*, than all the Vows I had made. It afforded, however, but a very small Portion of Contentment to either of us to know we were not Rivals in the same Affections, since such indissoluble Difficulties appear'd to oppose our Wishes, as left us not the least room to hope either would be able to obtain them.

For several Days *Zatilda*, as we had agreed, still keeping her Chamber: Her Indisposition was a tolerable Excuse for my putting off the Nuptials; but the Physicians appointed to attend her, giving in their Verdict that she was in Reality afflicted with no other Disease than Melancholy, not only my Father and *Mulyzeden*, who, for different Reasons, had all this while been sufficiently impatient, but also the King began to exert his Authority, and told me, That neither my Daughter's, not his own ill Humour, should any longer be a Pretence for affronting a *Prince*, whose Alliance was an Honour to all our Family. Judge what a Blow this was!—what a Crush to our Resolutions!—*Zatilda*, as soon as she was informed of it, cried out, *I am undone!—in spite of all you have promised me, in spite of your own distant Inclinations, you will be forc'd to be the* Prince's *Wife!* I was no less distracted, for Death would now have been less dreadful to me that *Mulyzeden's* Bed; yet, by what Means I should avoid it, without a plain Denial, and boldly daring the Rage of all those who had the Power over me, I could not, for the Soul of me, imagine. But *Passion*, when it is violent like mine, is never unaccompanied by *Courage*: I resolved rather to defy all Dangers, than yield to an Embrace, which even the *Idea* of was now grown odious, or make my dear *Zatilda* wretched, by utterly depriving her of even a Possibility of ever being otherwise. We pass'd our Hours for the most part together, not only because to talk of our mutual Misfortunes was all the Consolation that either of us enjoy'd, but also because I would avoid the Presence of *Mulyzeden* as much as possible; not but he sometimes visited her, but then he always sent to desire to know if he might have Permission, and I took care to retire into another Room, and by that Means escap'd the Persecution it was to me to hear his Complaints. This I did so often, and he being told by some of the Attendants that I was there, tho' he had not the Liberty of seeing me, that one Day he took an effectual Method to prevent me from concealing myself as I had done, without being guilty of a Rudeness unbecoming my Character:—He sent a Gentleman with his Duty to the two Princesses, who he knew were together, entreating the Favour of them to continue so, and allow of his Presence, having something to communicate to them both. My Cousin and I look'd on one another, while this Message was delivering, with a good deal of Surprise; but it being her Place to answer, she did in these Words: *Let your* Prince *know,* said she, *that I should take it ill if he should have so indifferent an Opinion of my Judgment, as not to assure himself of Welcome here, whenever he has a Leisure Hour to afford us his Conversation.—As for my* Cousin, *he is doubtless satisfied in her Inclinations.—Madam,* (interrupted I, affecting a gay Air,) *if he is not, I know of no Person on Earth so proper to complain to as yourself, who, on all Occasions, are so much his Friend.* I spoke this, because I knew that tho' he extremely respected her before, yet, since my deferring the Marriage, he had conceiv'd a secret Spite against her, as imagining, tho' for what Reason he could not dive into, she had been the Cause. And then addressing myself to the Person he had sent, told him, he might inform his Master, he had seen me with the *Princess,* where I design'd to remain sometime, and should be very well pleased if he would come and join Company with us; which he assuring us he would do immediately, withdrew.

Both *Zatilda* and myself were of Opinion, that the Business he had to communicate was no other than the old Story of my Unkindness, and growing more presuming, on the Part which the *King* seem'd to take in his Interest, sent in this particular Manner on purpose to oblige me to give him Audience, which of late, as I have already told you, I had avoided as much as possible. *Zatilda* was beginning to consider in what Manner she should answer him, in case he should desire her, as she imagin'd he would, to interest herself in this Affair, when he enter'd the Room: After the first Civilities were over, *Madam,* said he to me, *I have Reason to believe that Fortune having began her Persecutions to me in your cruel Coldness, designs to continue them in depriving me of everything which could afford me Consolation:* Abdomar, *that Friend, whom next to the adorable* Bellraizia *had the greatest Share in my Heart, of late avoids my Presence, shuns my Caresses, and when I ask the Cause, replies not but with Sighs. This Morning, pressing with all the Earnestness of Friendship, to which I joyn'd Commands, to know what had occasion'd this so sudden Change, after a thousand Evasions, which he found were vain, he told me with an*

*Accent which spoke at once Despair, and Grief, and Horror, his* Life *was mine, but not this* Secret. *I thought this Answer as far from* Justice, *as it was from* Kindness, *and let him know I had not been guilty of those Reserves to him, which, between Souls united, as I had believed ours, were treasonable to the Laws of Friendship. Our Tempers, both too liable to Passion, a few hot Words enflam'd, and he departed from my Chamber. This Usage, tho' it much troubles me, I could forgive from* Abdomar, *but he, it seems, is not so reconcileable. About an Hour since he sent a Letter by his* Page, *which please to judge his Meaning of.* In speaking these Words, he delivered me the Paper, which, at his Desire, I read aloud. The Contents of it struck me too deeply not to be fix'd in my Remembrance, and were in this Manner:

## To Prince MULYZEDEN

*My* Presence being no way serviceable to you in *Barbary,* and the Repose of my future Life calling me with the utmost Expectation to *Fez,* I humbly entreat your Permission to return thither. I know better what is owing to my Duty, and the Obligations you have heaped upon me, than to oppose your Will; but hope the same Goodness, to which I already stand so far engaged, will influence you not to command my Stay, since my immediate Departure is absolutely necessary to prevent me from being

The most Miserable of your Slaves,
ABDOMAR

The Concern which this unexpected Shock gave me, and which was impossible for me wholly to conceal, was not a little obliging to the unsuspecting *Mulyzeden,* who imagin'd it sprung only on his Account, especially when I told him, That I thought it the highest Piece of Ingratitude imaginable; and that he would be blam'd by the whole World for his too great Condescension, if he granted the Request he made: *What,* said I, *has he found so disobliging in the Court of* Barbary, *that should make him so impatient to remove from it? Or what Engagements can he have left behind him in* Fez *equal to those he has to his Prince, who has bought his utmost Services at a Price so noble as his Friendship.* Zatilda *join'd in all I said on this Score; but* Mulyzeden, who, in spite of his Resentment, had the most tender Friendship for him imaginable, tho' he could not but approve of our Reasons, could not be influenced by them so far as to *force* his Stay, if Perswasions would not win him. After a long Conversation he told me, he had a Favour to entreat of me, the Grant of which would infinitely oblige him; which having assur'd him I would, if in my Power, he inform'd me, That he believ'd it would not be improper if I seemed a little interested in this Affair, and took upon me to enquire of *Abdomar* the Reasons of his Desire to leave us. *Perhaps*, said he, *his Complaisance for a Princess of your Accomplishments may influence him to reveal more than I have been able to draw from him.* You may believe I did not hesitate much to promise what he desir'd: I was not a little satisfied to have an Opportunity of conversing so freely with *Abdomar*, and beginning to know what Jealousy inflicts, fancying it could be no other Reason than the Calls of Love, which made him regardless of everything beside, presently flatter'd myself with a secret Hope I should be able to discover something by his Words or Gestures which would give me Colour for opposing his Return.—I granted the Request which *Mulyzeden* made me with a Willingness which seem'd to banish Part of his Chagrin; and telling me he would send no Answer to *Abdomar* till I had first spoke to him, took his Leave with a Satisfaction much greater than I had seen in his Countenance since the Time of my first putting off the Marriage: But when his Absence had given me an Opportunity, how did I indulge Despair and Jealousy! how did I reproach *Zatilda* for accusing her ill Fate, since my own appeared by such infinite Degrees more dreadful! tho' as everyone looks on their own Misfortunes through a magnifying Glass, she could not be brought to yield me the Pre-eminence. Good part of the Night was pass'd in this kind of Conversation, and the Remainder in contemplating on the Intricacy of this Affair, which, indeed from the Beginning, promis'd nothing but Confusion. For my part, it had been many Nights since I knew what it was to sleep in Tranquility, but having this added to my other Disquiets, of losing, in all Probability, forever the Sight of all I wish'd to look on, fill'd me with such mortal Agonies, as the most elegant Descriptions of would make appear but mean in comparison of what in reality they were. Tir'd with my uneasy Bed, I rose much earlier than was my Custom; and because I would avoid the Morning Salutations which the *Court* though it their Duty to pay me, and which, with all other Formalities of State, were now grown troublesome, I went into the Palace-Garden without any Attendants, leaving Orders with them not to tell Prince *Mulyzeden*, my Father, or any other Person, where I was. It was not a Time for the Walks to be frequented, and I rambled up and down without being accosted by anyone, till growing a little weary, I went into a Grotto, which was order'd so, as to have many little Appartments in it, which run winding one out of another like a Labyrinth, and might entertain several Companies without being known by each other there. I was scarce set down, before I heard a murmuring Sound of Voices, that seemed in earnest Discourse; but whose they were, or what was the Subject of their Conversation, I was not able to distinguish. it is impossible for anyone to be less inquisitive into the Affairs of others than I am at all Times, but especially then, when I was so much taken up, and perplex'd with my own: I sat for some Moments without so much as a Thought what they might be, till one of them raising his Voice somewhat higher than he had done, I heard the Name of *Abdomar* repeated. That Sound, indeed, was sufficient to rouze me from a Lethargy, had I been in one. I left the Place I was in, and drawing nearer as softly as I could, soon found it was no other than he, whom Prince *Mulyzeden* had drawn thither on purpose to engage him to disclose the Secret he had been so desirous of knowing; for presently I heard him speak these Words: *Say no more*, Abdomar, (said he,) *say no more: I am now convinced that all the Friendship thou ever pretendest to me, was but to flatter me;—the Names of Prince, Patron, Friend, but Words of Course, and had no other Meaning than to please me with the Sound. Sir, I conjure you do not rend my Soul* (replied *Abdomar*) *with such unjust Suspicions; by Heaven, by all that we adore above, or the love below, your Friendship is the only Pride, the only Joy, the only Hope, I have on Earth; and when I forfeit that, I must be curs'd beyond my Enemies extremest Malice. Why then* (resum'd the Prince) *dost thou conceal this Secret from me? No, I never will believe thou lovest me, till I obtain this Proof.—I know too well thy honest generous Nature to imagine it can be ought thou would'st be asham'd to own; but if it were, to me thou might'st disclose it.—Humanity is liable to Failings, and if some stealing Vice has unawares crept into thy unguarded Wishes, I shall not conjure it with such Severity as thou thyself would'st do, having far more, and greater than my own.—O Sir, forbear,* (cry'd the other,) *you are too God-like good,—your wond'rous Condescension to an unworthy Slave makes me more hateful to myself.—Believe it, my most honour'd Prince, the Crime you would discover, is of so black a Kind, you cou'd not know it without Detestation: This once favour'd* Abdomar, *by you and by all Mankind must be contemn'd, abhorr'd; and if there were a Punishment more terrible, that,*

*that wou'd be inflicted on me. Thy Words* (interrupted *Mulyzeden*) *amazing as they are, can never make me think thou could'st be guilty of a Crime I cou'd not pardon. Hadst thou conspir'd against my Life, half this Penitence would more than wash the Stain:—But I will no farther press thee, keep still the Secret in thy burden'd Breast, but let me keep thee with me: Do not leave me, and I will ask no more. O unjust God!* (cry'd *Abdomar*, in a Voice that testified the utmost Horror) *why am I made this Wretch?—why doom'd to bear more than a mortal Sufferance can sustain?—why am I forc'd, against my Inclinations, to wrong such Royal Goodness?—Strike, strike me dead with your avenging Thunders!—Lightings blast me!—Earth open wide, and swallow me at once!—Snatch, snatch me, Fiends, and bear me quick to Hell!—There's not a Devil there so damn'd as I!—But hold,* (continu'd he,) *these Coward-like Complaints avail not to eraze my foul Ingratitude, my horrid Perjury:—I have the Means myself to end my Tortures, and chastise my Crimes. Thus, thus, my Prince, I will revenge you on your worst of Foes.*

With these Words, I was afterwards inform'd, he drew a Dagger from his Side, and was bout to plunge it in his Breast; but *Mulyzeden*, who, by the Beginning of those Exclamations, guess'd they would not cease without some Act of Desperation, was quick enough to prevent him; and wresting from him the fatal Weapon, spoke in a low and melancholy Accent, yet loud enough for me to understand what he said, in this Manner: *It is enough,* Abdomar, *it is enough; I need no more to make me guess at your Misfortune;—I am too well assur'd of your Honour to believe you wou'd injure a* Prince *who loves you, by any Act in which your Will had part:—No, no, the Crime which has occasion'd this Despair, is an involuntary one.—There are no Rules, alas! to limit* Love, *and I must learn to be insensible of* Bellraizia's *Charms, myself, before I refuse my Pity to another, who has felt their Influence.* Tho' I listen'd with all the Attention I was able, I cou'd not hear one Word after this for the Space of several Minutes; and when I did, it was in such broken Sentences, that had I not heard the *Beginning* of their Conversation, I cou'd have form'd no positive Judgment to what the *latter* Part of it tended, till *Mulyzeden,* who I found was about to leave him, spoke as he went out of the Grotto in this Manner: *Well,* Abdomar, said he, *I shall no more disturb you in the Enjoyment of a Solitude which you prefer to the Society of a Prince who loves you; only remember this, That there is a mighty Difference between Crimes enforced by a compulsive Fate, and those which we are guilty of merely thro' the Obstinacy of our own Will: The unhappy* Passion *you lament, is not your* Fault, *but your* Misfortune; *but if you offer to lay violent Hands on your own Life, you not only anticipate the Decrees of Heaven, but injure me in the most tender Part, by depriving me of a Subject I esteem the most capable of serving me, and commit a Sin unpardonable by the Gods and me.* By good Luck for me, who should have been strangely confus'd, had either the *Prince* or *Abdomar* known I had been Witness of this Discourse, the former went from the *Grotto* through another Passage, which led to a lower Garden, leaving that I was entirely free for me to retire, which I did, with all the Expedition I could, fearing lest *Abdomar*, who I found still continu'd where he was, should come out hastily and discover me. I walk'd a Turn or two in a fine green Alley adjoining to it, ruminating on what had past:—I cannot but say, it was an Infinity of Transport what I was eas'd of those Rackings of Jealousy which I had endured since I heard of his Impatience to return to *Fez*, and that so contrary to my Hopes and Expectations, he felt the same tumultuous Emotions which Desire creates, as had invaded me from the first Moment *Mulyzeden* brought him to my Presence; but then the Goodness, the Generosity of that unhappy *Prince*, injur'd by those in whom he most confided, reproach'd me with Ingratitude and Falshood: The Sense of his Suffering so truly touch'd me, that methought I could have done a Violence to my *own* Passion to have made him happy.— But then my Friendship to *Zatilda*, or I fancy'd it was that (because I was asham'd to own even to myself that *Love* had so far influenc'd me) which check'd the Growth of such an Inclination before I scarce could feel it rising in me. But to which of these two Motives it was my future Behaviour was owing, I will leave *Idalia* to the liberty of judging.

I had not long indulg'd in my Meditations, before I saw close by me the Person who took up the greatest Part of them: The half-distracted *Abdomar*, with Head declin'd, and folded Arms, had left the *Grotto*, and was coming down the Walk in which I was; the Confusion of both out Thoughts had prevented us from seeing one another till we were very near. The Start he gave at discovering me, sufficiently assured me he met me not with design, as did his offering, after he had made a low Bow, to turn away into another Walk: But my *Love* inspired me, at that Time, with a Boldness which I have a thousand Times since wondered at; and presently remembring the Request *Mulyzeden* had made me the Day before, resolved to make that my Excuse for entertaining the Man, for a Moment of whose Conversation I could almost have hazarded my Life: And calling after him,—*My Lord,* said I, *you do very wisely in*

*shunning the Presence of a Princess you are about so highly to disoblige. How!
Madam,* (cry'd the surpris'd *Abdomar,* endeavouring as much as possible
to throw of his Chagrin,) *were there a Possibility of my being guilty of a
Crime like that, I should deserve far worse than is in the Power of a Goodness
so divine as yours to inflict;—but since you have tax'd me with it, permit me
to entreat the Cause. The Cause is plain,* (resum'd I, counterfeiting a Gaiety
which was far from my Humour;) *if Prince* Mulyzeden *has not wrong'd
you in his Report, you grow weary of us, and are impatient to return
to* Fez. *The short Time I have been here* (reply'd he gravely) *has shewn me
so much to admire, that if there were a perfect Heaven to be found on Earth,
it is in the Court of* Barbary *I should seek it; and 'tis so much my Misfortune,
that I am oblig'd by an indispensible Necessity to leave it, that I much doubt
it never will be in my Power to eraze the Melancholy it occasions. Did you in
reality* think (said I) *what your Complaisance obliges you to* say, *no
Considerations would be of force to take you from a Prince who cannot be
happy when you are not with him. Abdomar* did not immediately make
any Answer to these Words; and I, who strictly obser'v all his Motions,
perceiv'd this Pause was occasion'd by the Suppression of some Sighs
which, endeavouring to vent themselves, has well nigh suffocated him;
but having at last got the Victory over them, *I am so little capable of being
serviceable to my Prince, Madam,* (said he,) *on any Score, that without
being guilty of an Injustice to himself, he cannot regret my Absence;—tho' if
it were otherwise, he will soon be put in Possession of a Blessing which will
leave no room for any second Wish: Whate'er* this World *can boast, cannot be
worth one Thought from him, who has all* Heaven *in the Divine* Bellraizia!
*But till that Day, at least* (answer'd I, smiling) *you ought not to forsake him,
and who can tell how long a Space of Time may be between this Instant
now, and that? You look with Wonder in your Countenance* (continu'd I,
perceiving him surpris'd;) *but knowing you so strictly devoted to you Prince,
I long have wish'd to discourse you on this Theme, and should be more oblig'd
than Words can thank you for, would you endeavour to divert his Thoughts
from one who cannot love him, nor but with Horror unconceivable can ever
yield to be his Wife.—Not* Love *him,* Madam! (interrupted he.) *Grant
Heaven my Ears deceive me!—not love a Prince who has all the Perfections
that Man can boast!—a Prince who dies for you! and to whom you have
given so many Assurances you would reward his Passion!—'Twas by my
Father's and the King's Commands,* (resum'd I;) *for know, my Heart had
never part in what I said, nor shall their Power oblige me longer to disguise
the Truth; I cannot love, and therefore will not consent it.—Hold,*

*Princess!* (cry'd the generous *Abdomar*, transported with Grief and Amazement,) *I conjure you by the Gods recal that rash Resolve, which else too late Consideration will enforce you to repent:—Where, in the Race of Man, can there be found a Worth like* Mulyzeden's? *The strictest Honour, Justice, Truth, and Goodness, are the Ingredients of his Godlike Soul! Then for his Form, O Princess! is it not noble?—What a manly Majesty dwells in his Air? What Sweetness in his Smiles?—And with all this, a Love so true, so perfect, and so pure, that which the Bless'd above regard each other with, is scarce so free from Taint.* Had I not been Witness of the Conversation which had lately pass'd between him and *Mulyzeden*, I should not have been surpriz'd to hear him plead in this Manner; but knowing him his Rival, the Generosity of his Soul fill'd me with a Wonder equal to my Love; and I must confess, tho' it was before at the greatest Height I them believ'd it could arrive, I felt from this Moment an Addition: But resolved to try him farther yet, *I own the Merits of Prince* Mulyzeden,(said I, coldly;) *but if you have ever been acquainted with that Passion, you well know that it is not without Reason that the God of it is painted blind. Ah! Madam,* (interrupted he,) *can you confess the least Knowledge what it is to love, yet seem insensible of it for* Mulyzeden's *Charms? But thus,* (continu'd he with an Accent which express'd the utmost Earnestness, and falling on his Knees,) *thus, most adorable* Bellraizia! *let me entreat you to consider well, e'er you resolve to make my Prince unhappy;—think what a Breach of Honour and of Justice it would be to throw him from those high-rais'd Hopes to which your Promises have exalted him;—think he cannot out live the cruel Certainty of your Unkindness; and if not* Love, *let* Pity *move you never to let this fatal Knowledge reach his Ear;—for me, not all the Tortures which the Damn'd endure should force me to reveal it.—Nor,—nor needst thou, Traytor!* (cry'd a Voice behind me,) *my Eyes and Ears have but too well inform'd themselves, and urge me thus to Vengeance.* With the hearing these Words, I saw the Person who spoke them was no other than Prince *Mulyzeden*, who, returning to the Palace, had been Witness of the Posture *Abdomar* was in; and drawing nearer as fast as he could, heard his last Words, which unhappily misconstruing, transported him so far as to make him draw his Sword, before the other had Time to put himself in any Posture of Defence, had he design'd it; but he attempted it not, and making bare his Breast when the Prince run fiercely at him, had certainly bury'd the Weapon in his Heart, had I not interpos'd. Frighted and confus'd as I was, I sent forth a Shriek which might have reach'd a much greater Distance, than it was to the Centinels which were placed at the Garden Gates, and stepping between them,—*Check this rash Sally of an ungovern'd and a causeless Fury*, (cry'd I to the Prince,) *or thro'* Bellraizia *give the Wound. You do well, Madam*, answer'd he, *to defend the Man who has declar'd a Passion for you, I wish that you had that Charity for all who love you. Your Words*, (resum'd I) *are too mysterious for me to comprehend the Meaning of, and all I can gather from them, or you Behaviour, is to* me *affrontive, and to your* Friend *injurious*. By this Time, there was a Crowd of Courtiers and Soldiers about us, and my *Father*, who happen'd to be just entring the Garden when I call'd out, came up among the rest: He had heard what I said to the Prince, and casting a furious Look at me, was about to speak, when *Mulyzeden* prevented him, by saying, *Sir, I desire you, whose* Authority *can justify the Act, as the Story which I have to tell you will my Accusation, to order that* Traytor (pointing to *Abdomar*) *into close Confinement, till a worse Punishment is inflicting on him*. My *Father* immediately making a Sign to some of the Guard, they took him away, which he submitted to with all the Resignation imaginable. I durst not utter the least Word of that Indignation my Soul was full of to *Mulyzeden*, because of my *Father's* Presence; but he walking away with the *Prince*, who was impatient to disburden his Bosom of the Anguish he was possess'd of, I went to *Zatilda's* Appartment to communicate to her this Adventure, and ask her Advice which way I should proceed; but I had scarce Time to recount it to her, before I receiv'd a Message from the *King* to retire to my own Side, and not to stir from thence without Permission.—Both the *Princess* and myself were extremely startled at this unexpected Mission; but the Person who brought it not leaving the Chamber till I went with him, neither of us had Opportunity to express what we thought.

After I was conducted to my Appartment, I found it was my Prison; the Persons who waited on me were order'd to admit no Persons without a particular Licence, nor deliver any Letter or Message for me without other Orders than my own. Incens'd to the greatest Vehemence my Temper could be rais'd to, at hearing this Command, I entreated to see my *Father;* but was told his Rage against me was too violent to permit me to come into his Presence, till he could bear it with more Calmness.—

As the charming *Bellraizia* was in this Part of her Story, she was interrupted by the sudden Rising of a Storm, which express the utmost Fury of the warring Elements: At first with distant Roar the whistling Winds but threaten'd Danger, but soon the dreadful, Noise came nearer;

from every Quarter of the angry Heavens the Tempest seem'd to blow, and demanded the Pilot's utmost Skill and Care: But soon there was no use of either; the horrible Hurricane baffled the Sailor's Art, and those who were adventurous enough to aim at stemming it, paid dearly for their vain Attempt.—At length, Masts, Cables, Rudder, all that could be defensive, being lost, the Ship was tost about at Pleasure of the mounting Waves, which sometimes bore it almost to the Skies, and sometimes dash'd it down so low, that those that were aboard had little Hope of rising.—A vast Variety of Horror might here be seen and heard, Numbers of distracted Wretches unfit either to live or die, but frighted at the Apprehensions of Death's near Approach, ran up and down confus'd, some cursing, some crying.—No Calm appeared but in the faces of *Abdomar*, and his *Bellraizia*, and they appear'd undaunted but for each other's Fate, and seem'd to comfort themselves, that since they must die, they should die together. As for *Idalia*, not all the Misfortunes she had endur'd, or the little Probability there was that Life should afford her any great Portion of Felicity, could enable her to support the Terror of this dreadful Hour; for it was not much more from the beginning of the Storm to the Time in which the Ship, bulging against a Rock, was dash'd to Pieces. Most of the Mariners, as expert as they were in swimming, perished in this watry Desolation; but *Idalia*, reserv'd to know more and greater Ills than yet she had endur'd, was miraculously preserv'd: In her Fright she had catch'd fast hold of one of the Beams which ribb'd the Side of the Ship, which being in the dreadful Crack torn off, she clinging round it, was plunged at once among the Waves. Who that had been Witness of this Scene would ever have believed they should have seen her alive on Shore? Yet it so pleas'd Providence, that the Storm, as though it had done the Work it was rais'd for, ceas'd immediately after, and the Piece of Timber lightly floating bore her to the Wreck of another Ship, which, like that she had been in, had suffer'd.—The broken Carcass lay tossing up and down, and stopp'd her further Progress. They were so near the Shore, that some People (as 'tis common for those who live by the Seaside) coming out in Boats either to enrich themselves by the Ruins of those who have perished, or to afford their Help to those who are in a Condition of receiving it, spy'd afar off with Wonder this little Log, which they discern'd bore something living on it, and made up to it with all the Speed their Oars enabled them: They arrived just Time enough to prevent *Idalia* and her Supporter from sinking, as else they must inevitably have done, suck'd into the Whirlpool which that unwieldy Wreck had made, and it was with all the Difficulty in the World, and danger to themselves, that they saved her. She was more dead than alive when they got her into the Boat; but rowing back again as soon as they could, one of the Men, who happened to be of a charitable and compassionate Disposition, carry'd her in his Arms to a little Cottage he had just by the Sea-side.—He had a Wife, whose Humanity and Goodness was much beyond what could be expected from People of their Station; she undress'd her, laid her on a Bed, and us'd the utmost of her Endeavours to bring her to herself, which at length she was successful in; and *Idalia* lifting up her Eyes, began to enquire where she was, and what happen'd; for she was capable of remembring nothing, since that dreadful Burst which tore her from her Company: Which when she had been inform'd of, and that in all Probability there was not a Person sav'd but herself, she was in the greatest Concern imaginable for the unhappy Fate of *Abdomar* and *Bellraizia*.

She continued some Days too weak to travel; and after she was in a Condition, could not resolve in what Manner: Her Beauty had led her into so many Dangers, that she resolved for the future to disguise her Sex till she should arrive at a Place of Safety; and persisting in her Design of going to *Naples*, thought her best Way would be through *Rome*, being now not above thirty Miles from thence. She had a String of Diamonds in her Hair the Day she left her Father's House, and on her putting on the Habit of a Country Girl to escape from the House where the unknown Person had plac'd her, she had ty'd it round her arm under her Sleeve; this she gave to the good old Host to sell, knowing it would be sufficient to pay him for his Trouble, and defray the Expences of her Journey.

The poor Fellow honestly discharg'd the Trust reposed in him, and brought her seven hundred Crowns; some part of which she dispos'd of in making him and his Wife a grateful Retribution for their Kindness and some of it she laid out in furnishing herself with Men's Clothes; the rest she kept to supply her in her Travels. But what befel her in them, and the Continuance of the Adventures of *Abdomar* and *Bellraizia* (who had not perished as she imagined) must be left for the next Part; which shall be the *last*, and fully conclude the History of this unhappy Wanderer.

*The End of the Second Part*

# Part III

How little are those blest with a paternal Protection, able to comprehend the thousand Dangers which attend a wandring and unguarded State of Life! The unhappy *Idalia*, accompany'd by that honest good-natur'd poor Fellow, who had preserved her from the Sea, had gone above half her Journey to *Rome* without meeting any Opposition; but happening to overtake three Gentlemen, who falling into Discourse with her on the Road, had told her, they were travelling that Way, she discharg'd her Guide, as believing she should have no further need of him. Her Men's Clothes, which she became exceeding well, she thought was Security enough from any of those Insults she had of late been so terrify'd with, and the Company of these Gentlemen from the Danger of losing her Way, or any other Inconvenience. But, alas! as much as she imagined she knew of the World, and as great a Variety of Adventures as she had gone through, she was now entring into a Misfortune she had not the least Notion of: She had not parted from her Conductor above a quarter of an Hour, before her new Companions began to ask her, what her Business was at *Rome*; how far she had travelled; the Names of her Parents; and a thousand other impertinent Questions, which she was now a little puzzled in what Manner to answer: But she thought there was no great Occasion for disguising the Story of her Shipwreck, therefore she gave them a brief Account of that; and as to the rest of the Enquires, only told them, That her Design was for *Naples*, but having suffered so much by the Uncertainty of the Weather, she chose rather to take so long a Journey by Land, than trust anymore to the Mercy of the Sea. They did not seem satisfy'd with this Reply, but press'd her very much to let them know to what Study she had been bred. *You appear*, said one of them, *to be a very pretty Youth; I cannot think you are of Quality, because you are without an Equipage, therefore must imagine your Education has been either for the Gown, or the Army. Doubtless it is so*, added the other, *and you have no Reason to conceal the Truth of your Affairs from us, who probably may be of Service to you. Ay*, resumed he that spoke first, *that we may, provided he has but Resolution. Hark ye*, (continued he, looking on *Idalia*,) *can you handle Arms?.—Have you ever learn'd to Fence?*—Interrogatories like these took from her all Capacity of answering! She grew both terrified and amazed, though she knew not the Cause, till one of them, who seemed to be the fiercest, gave her to understand they were of those who were called the *Banditti*, and that if she would consent to list herself among them, she would never want for anything. At this Information it was as much as she could do to keep herself from fainting away; but summoning all the little Spirit she had left, at last she had Courage to tell them, she had neither need, nor was fit for any such Employ: But that she thank'd them for their kind Intentions; and endeavoured to make her Refusal as civil as she could, fearing, and not without Reason, that Men who lived as they did, were not of a Humour to endure Plain-dealing. But all she could say, palliated not the Bitterness of her first Words, so much as to engage them to forgive the Contempt with which they found themselves treated; and one of them looking on this Fellow, presently cry'd, *Damn the little saucy Rascal, let us stick him against a Tree.—No*, (replied the other, who seem'd something more pitiful,) *let the foolish Boy live to repent his refusing so good an Offer; 'tis not worth our Trouble to kill him. Well then*, said the first, *we'll see what a Stock of Money he has that makes himself above societing with us, he shall help to support us without his Company. Ay, ay*, rejoin'd the other, *with all my Heart*.

Poor *Idalia* was too much frighted all this while to be able to utter one Word more, though by it she had been sure to save both her Life, and that which was now almost as precious to her, that little Money which had been raised on the last Thing she had of Value in the World, but suffered herself to be stripp'd of it without either entreating, or complaining. After they had ransacked her Pockets, they contented themselves with what they found there, and killing the Beast she rode on, (to prevent her making any Pursuit after them, in case any Persons should chance to come that Way, and join with her in it,) left her to get to *Rome* as she could.

It was sometime before the Terror this Accident had put her in, gave her leave even to reflect on the Misfortune that was befallen her; but when she did, scarce anything could seem more dreadful to her: Had they not destroyed her Horse, she might have hoped either to have found her Way to *Rome*, or someother Town, from whence she might have writ to *Venice* for a Supply; but to travel on Foot, was little agreeable to the Weakness and Delicacy of her Sex and Constitution: Besides, to be entirely destitute of Money in a Place so altogether unknown, was what might have shocked a Courage infinitely exceeding her's. She vented some Part of the Anguish of her Soul in Tears, but they unavailing to help her forward in her Journey, and the Necessity there was of prosecuting it, she at length rose from the Ground she had been sitting on, and began her weary Pilgrimage; the Thoughts of which, and the little Probability there was she should ever be able to go through it, render'd her yet more uncapable. She went on a slow Pace, yet too fast for her to continue long, and her Strength and Spirits failing, a thousand tormenting Considerations all at once assaulting her, Despair, which the natural Chearfulness of her Disposition had so often repelled, now seiz'd on her whole Soul; she yielded to the black *Idea* of her Woe, and thinking it Vain to struggle anymore against the o'erpowering Tide of strong Affliction, suffer'd herself to be born away with it, and for some Moments lost the Pain of *Thought*.—She was stretched at her Length in a kind of Slumber, or rather Fit, by the side of a little Stream which ran through a Meadow in sight of the great Road: Her Hat, when she lay down, had fallen off her Head, and her delicate Hair was blown by the Wind to and fro, now shading, now disclosing all her lovely Face to the Sun's burning View, who, if capable of those Desires which Poets have described him with, must have forsaken his *Car*, and stoop'd to be more blest than *Daphne*, had she been kind, could ever have made him.

It was in this Love and Pity-moving Posture she was discovered by a Lady; who passing by in her Chariot had seen something lie at that Distance, and had Curiosity enough to alight and walk to the Place where she was.—But when she beheld the Features of the beautiful *Idalia*, which neither the Fatigue, nor Fright, nor Grief she had endured could render unlovely, she began to feel a Trembling at her Heart, which she was too well acquainted with, not to comprehend: But not being of a Humour to constrain her Inclinations, indulged the growing Flame by gazing on, till the seeming *Chevalier* beginning a little to recover, looking up with Astonishment to see a Lady of a most dazzling Appearance, and attended by a Number of Servants in a Place where but a Moment before (as she imagined) she had been alone, and without Hope of meeting anybody, had such an additional Charm to what her sleeping Graces wore, that the already enflamed Lady, taking her for what her Dress bespoke her, was now half mad with wild Desires; but endeavouring to conceal her Sentiments from the Observation of her Servants, she turned to them, and being of a ready Invention, presently told them, that lovely Youth was one of her near Relations, and she supported by some Villany had been betray'd, and left there in that Manner. *Idalia* was enough come to herself to hear what she said, but had not Presence of Mind at that Juncture to determine how she should behave: At first she thought of discovering her Sex, believing it might be an Inducement to one of the same to afford her some Relief; but her speaking in that Manner to her Attendants, prevented her, and she remained silent, as not being able to guess what 'twas she meant, till the Lady asking her how she came to be alone; and in a Disorder which was visible in her Face, she told her she had been in the Hands of Robbers, who had left her nothing but her Life. *Thank Heaven for that*, said the enamoured Lady, *all other Misfortunes may be redeem'd; and since I know you are a great Way from your own Home, be pleas'd to accept of mine for sometime: My House is not above three Miles distant from hence; I have a Chariot waits, and you shall go with me to take that Repose which the Condition I find you in seems to require.* Idalia had not the Power of answering her any otherwise than with a low Bow, so much had one Surprise on the Back of another depriv'd her of her wonted Readiness of Apprehension; but thinking whatever Design this unknown Lady had, either in the Civilities she shew'd her, or the Tale she had invented of her being a Relation, it could not be anything to her Prejudice, or if it were, it was still shifting the Scene of Vexation, which to the Wretched is some Ease, she gave her Hand, and suffered her to lead her to the Chariot; where as soon as they were seated, *I perceive*, said the Lady, *that you are surpris'd at what I told my Servants; but it was a Stratagem which my Prudence inspir'd me with: My Pity to see a Person of your Appearance in so dejected a Posture, first led me to a Resolution to remedy your misfortunes, if it be in my Power; and the Regard every Woman ought to have for her Reputation, join'd to the common Safety of us both, to make you pass as a Relation, lest at the Return of my Husband, who is now Absent, and will be for some Days, my Behaviour should be reported to him in a different Manner from what I would have it.—There is*, continued she *a curs'd Necessity in Wedlock, which obliges one sometimes to disguise the Truth, and for that Reason Fools should never Marry.* These Words, and the Air which accompany'd them, made the pretended *Chevalier* guess to what Motive she was indebted for this unexpected Relief, and in spite of the various Disquiets which possess'd her, could scarce forbear smiling to herself at the Oddness of such an Adventure; but thinking it could not be to her Detriment to humour the Caprice, and having too well been acquainted with what Men say on those Occasions, answered her in Terms which were infinitely obliging to her. Donna *Antonia* (for that was the Name of this Lady) already began to flatter herself with a Belief she was secure of the Heart of this Young Charmer; and free from all those Fears which generally are the Companions of Love, talk'd all the Way with as much Familiarity as tho' their Acquaintance had bore the Date of many as Years as it did of Minutes; But desiring to be inform'd of the Name and Quality of her Lover, our little *Hero* presently told her, That though there were some Reasons which obliged him to conceal himself, yet that he should make no Scruple of letting her know both who he was, and why he left the Place of his Birth: And then related a long Account, which she form'd in the speaking, That she was born at *Verona* of one of the most noble Families in the Place; but, having the Misfortune to kill in a Duel of a Son of one of the Magistrates, was obliged to fly till the Affair could be made up. *This, Madam*, said the counterfeit Don, *is my History, nor have I anything farther to inform you of, than that in my Way to* Rome *I met some of the* Banditti, *who have plundered me of all the ready Money, Jewels, and Bills, I had about me, leaving me in the Condition in which your Compassion found me, without anything to recommend me to your Care, but a Heart entirely free from all Engagements except those which the Influence of your Charms has made.* In fine, the little Gallant address'd in a Fashion so agreeable to the Sex she imitated, that it was no Wonder Donna *Antonia* was both deceived and charmed with it. When they came to the End of their Journey, they alighted at the Gate of a magnificent Dwelling, which being open'd, our young Adventurer was conducted in with all imaginable Ceremony; a fine Collation was immediately set forth, where the richest Wines, choicest Fruits, and extravagant Kindness of the fair Inviter, strove which most should please the beloved Guest: But, alas! whatever Smiles her Face might be constrain'd to wear, her Heart felt little Satisfaction in all the Splendor she saw about her, and the Welcome she found: She long'd with the utmost Impatience to be alone, and at liberty to indulge a Melancholy she had but too just a Cause for; Fatigue, entreated she might retire. *Antonia* willing to oblige her Favorite in all Things, deny'd herself the Pleasure of his Conversation to allow him that of his Repose, and ordered him to be shewed to a Chamber, one of the noblest in the House.

Idalia had been so much accustomed to the Vicissitudes of Fortune, that she was less astonish'd at this, than probably another would have been: But it serv'd very much to encrease the Perplexities she was in. She knew not whether to consider it as a good or ill Chance: To be relieved from the Fear of perishing in so miserable a Manner as that of

Want, she could not but acknowledge as a peculiar Mark of the Care of an All-seeing Providence; but then the Passion, which the Mistake of her Sex had inspir'd in the Person ordain'd to be her Deliverer, she thought an *Omen* of something fatal to her, though she could by no means form any Conjecture by what Means, Full of melancholy Reflections of the Dangers, the Terrors, the Disappointments she had met, and those which in all likelihood she was yet to encounter, she fancied she regretted the unaccountable Obstacles which had hitherto hindered her from a monastick Life, the most of any Misfortune she had gone through; but, alas! how little was she capable of judging of her own Soul!—The Remembrance of *Myrtano's* Charms,—the swelling Transports whenever Imagination presented him to her, with those tender Wishes, in his Eyes, which often she had read there,— the Horror which invaded her, when she reflected on his Infidelity,— would soon have made her sensible in any other's Case, that it was to the Temple of *Love* the chiefest of her Orisons were directed, and *Religion* had but the second Place. But however it were, never Woman endured more through the working of so many different Passions; and it was the Confusion of her Thoughts alone that render'd her incapable of forming, much less of keeping any Resolution Reason should suggest. It certainly had been the most prudent, as well as most honourable Part, to have confess'd herself a Woman to Donna *Antonia*; but the Uncertainty what she should do, or where to retreat, if by that Discovery she should forfeit her Protection, deterr'd her from it. The Perturbations of her Mind, which hinder'd her from closing her Eyes all Night, the cast Fatigue she had endur'd in walking so much beyond her Strength, together with a Cold she had got by lying on the Grass, threw her into a Fever; which as soon as *Antonia* was inform'd of by the Servant whom she sent with a Good-morrow, she ordered a Physician immediately to give his Attendance; all imaginable Care was taken, nor could there have been more, had the Welfare of the whole World depended on this single Life.—What Zeal, what Caution, what Tenderness, does Love inspire, when alarmed with the least Dander of losing the beloved Object! *Antonia* would needs be present at every Prescription, trusted no Hand but her own to mingle up the Medicines, watch'd herself by the Bedside, and chid the tardy Nurse's Sloth, listen'd to every Groan, and answer'd them with Sighs. Never did the fondest Wife, the tenderest Mother, or most dutiful Child, with such unfeigned Concern, such interested Hopes and Fears, alternate Joy and Terror, everyday, almost every Hour, receive the different Sentiments which the Physicians gave, according as the Distemper abated or encreas'd. For several Days no settled Judgment could be made of Life or Death; but at last, the Strength of Nature in so young a Person, joined to the extraordinary Care and Skill which had been us'd, o'ercame the Malignity of the Disease, and she was transported with the News, that her dear Cousin (for so she call'd the feign'd *Chevalier*) was entirely out of Danger.

But this Indisposition had made a very great Alteration in the Sentiments of *Idalia*; for as before she but fancy'd she wish'd for a *Recluse* Life, she now in reality began to do so; with her bodily Strength, her Passions were now debilitated, the Noise and Hurry of the World were now in good earnest odious to her, and Love itself, though not wholly extinguish'd, burned with a dim and feeble Fire: The Duties of Religion, and a true Repentance for the Mismanagement and Follies of her past Life, now took up all her Thoughts; and as she was of a Disposition generous enough, when Vanity, Pride, or Love, did not oversway her, she resolved to undeceive *Antonia*, and use the utmost of her Endeavours to perswade her to turn the Current of her Affections, where both the Laws of God and Man required them, and henceforward banish all Desire but for her Husband. She had just fix'd herself in this pious Resolution, when *Antonia* came into the Chamber; and before she could have an Opportunity of executing it, told her, the Reason she had absented herself so lone, (for she had not been there in some Hours,) was, That her Husband was returned from *Viterbo*, where he had been sometime before her Arrival, and that in Decency she had been oblig'd to Dine with him; but having told him, she had a near Relation in the House, he desir'd, if it was not inconsistent with his Repose, to be admitted to visit him. What *Idalia* had to say would have taken up more Time than could now be spar'd; besides, she was willing to see what the Person and Behaviour of this Gentleman would allow her to say in his Favour, before she attempted to work any Change in the Sentiments of his Wife: Therefore only telling her she should receive the Favour he intended her with that Pleasure which became one so much oblig'd, *Antonia* took her Leave with a Smile, which testified it was not to him he had been obliged, and immediately returned accompanied by her Husband.

Idalia, by reason of her Weakness, still kept her Bed, but was supported by Pillows in such a Manner, that she rather *sat* than *lay*: She had compos'd her Mind as much as possible, that she might be the

ELIZA HAYWOOD

better able to make a Judgment of this Gentleman. But how immediately was it o'erthrown!—how, in an Instant, was all the Sedateness she had assum'd chang'd into Confusion, Shame, Horror, Distraction, when the Moment they enter'd the Room she saw the Husband of *Antonia* was no other than *Myrtano*!

What Words, can represent, what Heart conceive what hers endured at this so unexpected, so shocking a View! A thousand Furies all at once possess'd her, chill Fear and burning Rage, wild Jealousy and mad Despair, and Thought-disjointing Amazement, with all the black *Ideas* they could raise, crowed into her Soul.—Of all the surprising Accidents of her unhappy Life, nothing is more to be wondered at, than that she survived this dreadful Moment, or at least did not by some Extravagance discover both her Sex, and the Cause of her Distraction: But though her Eyes shot perfect Fires, and seem'd to start from forth their glowing Orbs,—her Lips trembled, her Hair stood at an end as though some Spectre had met her Sight, and every Limb was shook with inward Agonies, yet she neither spoke, not acted anything which could give the Standers-by the liberty of guessing from what Cause the Alteration they beheld had sprung. *Antonia* appeared infinitely troubled to find so sudden a Change, which she looked on as a Relapse into that Distemper which had given her so many Fears; and *Myrtano's* Good-Nature and Complaisance oblig'd him to join in her Concern. They perceived the Stranger was not in a Condition to endure Company, and *Antonia* ran instantly away to send for the Physician.

Had they stay'd longer, 'tis probably indeed she might not have had the Power of preserving herself undiscovered; for it was not to any Presence of Mind that her Reserve was owing, but to the too great Multitude of various Emotions, which, warning with each other in her Bosom, would not suffer her to utter any.—She fell into a Swoon the Moment they left the Room, and by that Means was very near discover'd to the old Nurse that attended her, that her Patient was not of the Sex she pretended to be; for after rubbing her Temples, and applying Things to her Nostrils, she was about to open her Linnen Wastecoat, which she had always wore close button'd, just as she recovered: But her *ill Genius* had prevailed so far over her *good one*, as not to suffer the Discovery to be made in a Manner so little to her Prejudice, as also to prolong her Life, to experience more Misery: In spite of her Weakness, in spite of the additional Torments the Sight of *Myrtano*, as Husband of *Antonia*, had inflicted on her, she grew better everyday, and in a

Week's Time was able to walk about her Chamber: All which Time she was visited sever Times in a Day by the fair Wife of Don *Myrtano*, who in spite of the Caution she had of giving him any Suspicion of her Inclinations, could not forbear gratifying them so far as to come as often as she could get an Opportunity, to look upon her Soul's Ador'd. But the Sentiments of *Idalia* were now entirely chang'd again; she no longer thought it proper to make herself be known, not could find in her Heart to use any Endeavours for the Conversion of *Antonia*; she rather wished her Indifference for him might encrease; for since she knew her to be a Rival, and a Rival possess'd of all those Joys she once had vainly hoped, not all the good Offices she had done her could hinder her from regarding her with a mortal Hatred.—Him too she hated, or she imagin'd at that Time she did so; and if in the wild Tumults of her troubled Thoughts she ever was compos'd enough to pray, it was only to invoke Heaven to revenge her Wrongs, and curse them both with lasting Discord and eternal Strife.

All the Time of her keeping her Chamber, *Myrtano* had never offered to visit her since the first Time; at which she was not a little astonished, and began to fear that even in that transient View he had seen enough through her Disguise to know her; and conscious of the Injustice he had been guilty of to her, was asham'd to meet the Reproaches of her Eyes.— *Antonia* was also surprised, but would not press it, nor ask the Reason of his Neglect, least he should imagine her, as she was, too far interested in it; and having by his Absence greater Opportunities of entertaining her Beloved, did not much perplex herself about finding out the Meaning of his allowing her to do so. She was infinitely more concern'd, that the Darling of her Wishes had made so small a Return to her Advances: The seeming Youth had behaved himself with so much Gallantry the Day she brought him home, that she expected an immediate Declaration of Affection would have ensued. All the Time of his Sickness she had no other Fear than to be deprived of her Desires by Death; but now, when she perceiv'd him perfectly past Danger, she found herself farther from the Possession of them than ever she had believ'd herself; and one Day being alone in the Chamber with him, could no longer contain the furious Ardour with which she was possess'd, but not only by her Words, but also Actions, endeavour'd to make the dear Ungrateful sensible how much she had suffer'd from his Coldness.

Idalia, who hated her before for being the Wife of *Myrtano*, now despis'd and scorn'd her; the endearing Expressions with which she was treated by her, made her appear more odious; and wholly unguarded by the Multiplicity of her Reflections, before she was aware, flinging away, and stamping, *Gods! Gods!* cried she, *is this a Woman for* Myrtano *to love?* She had no sooner spoke these Words, than he rush'd into the Room with his Sword drawn, and had certainly prevented her from ever saying more, if his Wife, as much surpris'd as she was, had not been quick enough to prevent him, by catching fast hold of his Arm, and continuing to hang upon it, notwithstanding all his Endeavours to throw her off; *Begone, perfidious Woman*, said he furiously, *unless you wish to perish, with your* Minion, *a Victim to your shameful Passion. Is it not enough that you conspir'd the Death of her who alone was worthy of my Love, but you must add Adultery to your Design of Murder?—You know I am not ignorant of your monstrous,—your more than brutal Disposition:—Howe dare you then to tempt me thus, lest I should take a full Revenge for all my Wrongs at once? I never, never wrong'd you*, (interrupted she, still clinging fast about him:) *if I contriv'd my Rival's Death, 'twas Love of you that was the Cause, inhuman Man as you are to upbraid me with it. And was it Love of me* (resum'd he, more violently) *that induc'd you to court this Stranger, whom falsly you would have pass'd on me for a Relation?—But I have been inform'd of all, and will have Reparation.* In speaking these Words, he us'd his utmost Force to disengage himself, and having done it, ran fiercely at *Idalia*; which she perceiving, evaded the Blow by falling on her Knees; and imagining something by the Reproaches which in his Indignation he had made his Wife, prevented him from lifting up his Hand against her, by crying out to him, *Hold, hold, Don* Myrtano, *I conjure you spare my Life till you shall know who 'tis you are about to destroy, and till you satisfy me who that Lady was, your Wife so cruelly design'd to murder. What is that to thee?* (resum'd he, vex'd that he had mention'd that before him.) *Oh! 'tis of more Moment,* (answer'd she,) *perhaps, to you and me, than yet you comprehend.—For Heaven's sake then, and for your own, indulge my Curiosity in this Request, and tell me, if the Lady destin'd to fall a Sacrifice to you and Love was not call'd* Idalia?—Both the Husband and the Wife started from their Places they stood in at the Mention of that Name, as tho' a Clap of Thunder had pronounced it; but the former looking earnestly in the Face of the Person that spoke it for the space of two or three Minutes, found something there that dissipated great Part of the Fury that he had been in: The Air, the Features, and the Voice of *Idalia* were too deeply imprinted in his Memory not to be distinguish'd thro' all Disguises. Immediately he knew her, and regardless of his Wife's Presence, flew to her, and caught her in his Arms, and cried in an Extasy which no false Lover could feign *It is, it is* Idalia *my only everlasting Charmer.*

It was impossible for a Woman, who lov'd with that Transcendency of Passion, to be thus clasp'd yet feel no Satisfaction in the tender Pressure: Not all the Resentment she had against him for his marrying another, had Power to made her resist his Embraces; but as soon as he had given them Truce, which he did only to gratify his Sight with another View of her dear well-known Face, as he had done his Touch in holding her to his Bosom, she recollected herself enough to remove some few Steps from him; and looking on him with a Countenance as severe as she had Power to put on,—*I was satisfied you should know who I am*, (said she,) *because you should be sensible how little your Wife has been capable of wronging you in the Manner your jealous Fury had suggested; but desire not, as you are now another's, any Testimonies of that former Affection which was between us, which you have forfeited, and I am willing to forget, since the Remembrance would be as great a Crime in me, as that you lately suspected her guilty of.* He was just going to reply, when Donna *Antonia*, who had all this while been unable, by reason of her Surprise, to discharge any Part of the Rage she was full of, stepping hastily between them, cried, *And are you* Idalia? *Yes*, (answer'd she, not at all daunted at the Fury she saw in her Countenance;) *and I imagine you are the Niece of the Count* Miramont. 'Tis probable here might have follow'd a Combat of Words, the War of Women, if Don *Myrtano* had not put an End to it. *Madam*, (said he to his Wife, in a Voice nothing soften'd from that in which he had spoke to her before,) *tho' I am assur'd no Injury could here be done me, yet your Intentions were the same. My own Ears heard you declare a Passion shameful to your Sex and Character; but it is hereafter that I shall tell you my Sentiments on this Affair. In the mean Time I command you, by that Power the Name of Husband gives me, (and which your forfeiting all Title) either retire to your own Apartment, and wait my Coming. This*, (continued he more sternly, perceiving her not about to go,) *if you refuse to obey, I will this Moment make Complaints of your Behaviour to the* Pope *and lay before him the whole Scene of your Proceedings.* Of as haughty and impatient a Disposition as *Antonia* was, this Menace exacted her Complaisance; and she left the Room, only casting a Look back on *Idalia*, which spoke, more plainly than a thousand Words could do, the Violence of her Rage.

ELIZA HAYWOOD

The Reader will easily imagine, that after she was gone, Don *Myrtano* addressed his long-lost Charmer with all the soft Endearments suitable too so surprising an Occasion; but she, who was not willing to yield to the Pleasure she took in hearing them, and withal desirous to be inform'd by what means Donna *Antonia* had known her to have been her Rival, it being a Secret she believ'd too all in *Venice*, and also if it were really she who had brib'd the *unknown Person* to murder her in the Forest, let him know it would be more satisfactory to her to be let into what he knew of these Affairs, than all he could say on any other. He was too glad of an Opportunity, which, while he obliged her in the Grant of her Request, would also clear him of his suspected Infidelity, to let it slip; and engaging her to sit down by him, while he fulfilled her Commands, began to unravel a Mystery, which had appeared so confounding to her Understanding, in these Words:

*The History of Don* Myrtano, *and Don*
Honorius dell Miramont.

You may remember, Madam! *(said he, sighing)*, doubtless with an Infinity of Indignation remember, that the last Time I ever had the Blessing of seeing you at *Vicenza*, I receiv'd not the Honour you then vouchsafed me, of assuring me you would not refuse to be mine, when ever I should claim you by Ways you should approve, and as became a Man worthy of the adorable *Idalia's* Affection: But, oh! had you been sensible what I endur'd in the severe Necessity of appearing so ungrateful, so stupid, so blind to the inestimable Happiness that Condescension offer'd me, you would rather Pity than condemn me—I had, when I was very young, been contracted by my Parents to Donna *Antonia dell Miramont*, she who is now my Wife; and who, being bred here at *Rome*, I had never seen: But a former Intimacy between our Families was the Occasion of this, which I must now call unhappy *Union*. For my part, as I had a Heart entirely unprepossessed, I agreed to it without any manner of Reluctance, but had not Complaisance enough to take a Journey to visit her: The Count her Uncle, perhaps, imagining the Sight of her might engage me to hasten the Consummation of the Contract, sent her to *Venice* with an Equipage and Train proportion'd to the Fondness he had for her. At her Arrival I thought her very agreeable to what I then wish'd for in a Wife, and indeed lik'd her better than any Lady I had seen; nay, I really loved her enough to be impatient for the

Celebration of the Nuptials, and accordingly ordered everything to be prepared for it. The Day was appointed; and it was that in which my unhappy Brother and Don *Ferdinand* fell Rival Victims to Love and your Almighty Charms. Decency forbad the *Hymeneal* Torch should mingle with the *Funeral* Taper, and the Wedding by Consent of both Parties was deterr'd. A fatal Curiosity inclining me to see those Eyes, those lovely Orbs of shining Ruin, I no longer thought *Antonia* worth my Care; but I need not tell you how much I lov'd, how much I ador'd an Excellence so far beyond all that ever was called Mortal, a thousand, thousand Times you have read it in my Eyes!—These glowing burning Balls, which never gaz'd upon you without starting, and almost breaking the Strings which held them with Extasy unspeakable!—with Pleasure would up to such a height of racking Rapture, that it even became a Pain, and stagger'd Sense!—O, what would I not then have given to have had it in my Power to offer you a Passion worthy of your Acceptance!—How did I curse my Engagement with *Antonia?*—How many Stratagems did I invent to break with her? But she, better acquainted with the Secret of my Soul than at that Time I imagined, artfully evaded my Excuses, and circumvented me in all, either because she then had really an Affection for me, or, as 'tis most probably by her Conduct since, thought it would be a Reflection on the Power of her Beauty to have it said, she had come so far to marry a Man who on any Terms could be brought to forsake her.—In fine, let me do what I would, say what I would, she seem'd not to resent it; and render'd it an Impossibility for me to quit her, without making myself appear the most ungrateful and perfidious of Mankind.—I was in this perplexing *Dilemma*, when you made Tryal of my Faith, by proposing what I would have given my Soul to have had it in my Power to accept.—I am sure you cannot forget the Constitution which was too visible in my Countenance not to be observed, which perhaps you might impute to another Score, but was really occasioned only by the inward working of my tumultuous Desires, which long'd with an Ardency inexpressible to satisfy you in a Demand which would have been so glorious for me; yet I knew not how I should effect it, though a Multitude of Inventions crowded that Moment at once into my Head, and flatter'd me with some little Hopes.—I went, you know, immediately away; which haste proceeded from my Impatience to return with Tydings more suitable to my Passion to bring, than any I had yet been able to tell you.—Alas! I little thought 'twould be so long before we met again, not of the Treachery which was then in Agitation to separate us forever:—But of that hereafter.—

When I had put in Execution all the Stratagems my Passion for you inspired me with, and found them fruitless to work the Effect I wish'd,—I had no longer Patience, but resolved at my next Visit to disclose to you the whole History of my Misfortune: On the Road to *Vicenza*, about four Miles distant from my own *Villa*, I saw a Horse standing still; and looking down on a Person who lay on the Ground by him, I presently imagin'd it was somebody who had either suffer'd by a Fall from that Horse, or the Villany of some Robbers: But drawing nearer to offer what Assistance was in the Power of myself or Servants to afford, I heard him utter most piteous Lamentations, mixed with Groans.—Both Christianity and common Compassion obliges those of the highest Rank of Life to do what good Offices they can, even to the meanest; and though this Man appeared to be one of those, I should have thought it a Pride no way commendable to have trusted the Belief of his Misery to any Care but my own: I immediately alighted, and raising him a little, presently discover'd, (to my great Surprise, to find him in such a Posture and Habit) the Face of Don *Honorius dell Miramont*, the Brother of *Antonia*, and without Exception, a Chevalier of the most Perfections I ever found in Man.

*Idalia* could not here forbear interrupting him, to let him know he might spare himself the Trouble off giving any Character of that accomplish'd young Nobleman; for she was perfectly acquainted with his Worth, having the Honour of being frequently in his Company at *Venice*.

*Yes, Madam!* (resumed Don *Myrtano*) *I am sensible you have seen him, and that the Consequence of such Interviews have been such as you never fail of causing,—to inspire a Passion too just to be oppos'd by Reason, and too violent to suffer any Considerations to be of force to overcome it.* But (*continued he*) to pursue the little History I am about to give you, this unhappy Gentleman, who seemed in Agonies such as seizes on the Body when the Soul is departing from it, no sooner cast his Eyes upon me, than he cry'd out, *O Don* Myrtano, *you come in happy Time to revenge my Death!—I am poisoned!—the fatal Dose was given me by* Ardella.—A sudden Pang seizing him that Moment, prevented his saying anymore for sometime; and I, who perceiv'd his Condition was indeed deplorable, though it now a Season to talk, but act, if there were any Means which Art or Nature could furnish to repel the Malignity of the Poison; and immediately dispatched one of my Servants to *Villa Rica* for a *Litter*, and another to *Padua*, to order a Physician, who I knew was a most skilfil one, to meet us at *Vicenza* with all possible Expedition; the third, for by good Fortune I had so many with me, took Care of my Horse while I kneel'd down by the agoniz'd *Honorius*, and by holding his Sides, and sometimes his Head, according to the carious Shootings of his Pain, afforded him some little Ease. I was impatient to the last Degree, to know what he meant by saying my Servant *Ardella* had given him the Poison, and fancied him to be a little delirious with the excessive Torture he endured, till having a little Respite from it, he again said, That it was she who had administred it to him, but that he very well knew it was to oblige another she had done so. These Words gave me Apprehension that he might imagine it occasioned by my Order, and I was beginning to protest my Innocence; but he perceiving my Intent, cry'd out to me to speak no more, for he was well assured I was both innocent and ignorant of any such Thing: *But*, continued he, *I know not if you will afford me any Pity for my Sufferings, when you shall be told the Injury I have done you: But we are neither of us exempt from Faults; and you must pardon me, as you would wish to be forgiven by those to whom you are guilty of Injustice.*—There was something so mysterious in these last Words, that I could not possibly dive into their Meaning; and the violence of his Pain returning, prevented me from desiring him to make an Explanation of them, till another small Cessation happening, he did it of his own accord in the Manner:

You must know, *said he*, that in all her Pride of Innocence I happened at a Ball to dance with the admired *Idalia*, and from that Moment was inspir'd with a Passion for her, which not all her late Misfortunes, which have made so great a Noise at *Venice*, could eraze. I was just determined to urge my Suit to Don *Bernardo's* Ears, when her sudden Absence from his House prevented me; since which, though I have searched for her with a Diligence proportioned to the Love I had for her, I never could hear the least Tittle to what Place, or with what happy Man she was retir'd, till my Sister's Jealousy of you furnished her with Means to inform me, without knowing, at the same Time, how much she obliged me in it: But coming one Day to visit her, I found her drown'd in Tears; which enquiring the Reason of, she told me, You had of late very much degenerated from the Affection you once professed, and which the Engagements between you demanded the Continuance of. She presently took it in her Head, that there must be some Rival in the Way; and imagining she was either at *Vicenza*, or near that Place, because she had observed you past most of your Time there, contrary to your Custom; and resolving to satisfy her jealous Curiosity, found out a Method which nothing but the subtil-working Wit of an impatient disappointed Woman could suggest: She got acquainted with a Sister of *Ardella's*, (who, by some Accident she had heard, was a sort of Housekeeper to you at *Vicenza*,) and by her Means with herself: by Promises and Bribes she engaged that mercenary Wench to her Interest, and won the whole Secret from her of *Idalia's* having been from the Time she left *Venice* a Guest there, first to Don *Henriquez*, and afterwards to you.

Such a Discovery was, I confess, sufficient to alarm a Heart much less imperious than *Antonia's*; but having as great a Share of *Cunning* as *Pride*, would take not the least Notice to you that she had any jealous Sentiments, much less that she was pris'd of anything which could raise them. When she gave me this Account, she little imagined I had any further Interest in it, than the Part which Nature oblig'd me to take for a Sister affronted in this Manner; but tho' I was not without that Consideration also, yet the Affection I had for *Idalia*, and the Misfortune I thought it to have her in your Possession, had infinitely the Pre-eminence, and I presently form'd a Contrivance of dressing me in the Fashion you see, and went to *Vicenza*; where lurking about the House, I was in hopes of seeing her, or at least hearing something more than yet I had been informed off. But Fortune favoured me not so far; I had been there several Days before anything accrued to my Observation: But what added to my Disquiet the Sight of you twice entring, and the Imagination what a Prodigality of Felicity you were going to enjoy in the Society of *Idalia*, made me almost wild. But at last I found an Opportunity of getting into the Company of *Ardella*, and by the Character my Sister had given of her sordid Disposition, knowing which way to ingratiate myself, made her Presents of some little Trifles, which I bought of a Fellow who I saw offering them to Sale: They were such as were suitable to the Appearance of the Person who gave them, and tho' of very small Value, were acceptable to this greedy Creature; and I soon became so great with her, that I flattered myself I should in a little Time be Master of the whole Secret of *Idalia*. Complaining that I was in Distress for a Lodging while I stay'd at *Vicenza*, she made me an Invitation of lying in your House till I had finished the Business which I pretended had brought me to that Part of the Country. You need not doubt but I accepted of an Offer so obliging to my Wishes, assuring myself I should now have an opportunity of both seeing and speaking to my ador'd *Idalia*, to whom I resolved, let the Consequence be what it would, to discover who I was; if she was detained there against her Inclinations, as sometimes the good Opinion I had of her led me to believe, I design'd to bear her off, tho' with the Hazard of my Life; or if it were thro' Choice she had continu'd with you, to endeavour, by all the Arguments I was Master of, to perswade her to remove.—But, alas! my Expectations in this, as in all other Things, were frustrated; tho' I was in the House several Days, she kept so close in her Appartment, it was impossible for me even to get a Glimpse of her: And I was beginning to despair I ever should be so bless'd, when as I was sitting in the Hall, meditating to what little Purpose was all the Pains I had taken, *Ardella* came to me, and bidding me follow her into the Garden, led me to that Part of it which was most remote from the House, and taking me by the Hand, *Banno*, (said she, for that was the Name I went by,) *you pretend a great deal of Friendship to me, what would you do to* prove *the Reality of what you have profess'd?*

You may imagine I was not a little surpris'd at her speaking in this Manner; but soon recollected myself enough to assure her, I would do anything in my Power. *What I have to desire of you*, (resumed she,) *will not only be an Obligation to me, but also to yourself, if you are but possess'd of two Qualities necessary for the Undertaking; they are Secrecy and Resolution: Therefore, before you promise, examine your own Heart, whether there is anything in it which would tremble at the Performance of a Deed, perhaps, such as the World calls by the Name of bloody,—cruel,—barbarous, and such-like Epithets, invented only to fright the Ignorant from accomplishing their Wishes, and cheat us into tame Enduring:—Weigh well, if you can boldly make your Fortune by one brave Blow, without a childish Repentance afterwards, which would undo both yourself, and those by whom you are employ'd.* I was too impatient to know what 'twas she meant to hesitate much what Answer to make, but immediately promis'd to stick at nothing, not thinking myself oblig'd to a Performance, if it were either inconsistent with my Honour, or Interest.—My ready Compliance made her take me for such a one as she wanted; and shewing me a Purse of Gold, *Look here!* said she, *all this is yours to encourage you in the Undertaking; but there are three Times as much in store for you when you bring Word 'tis done:—But let me know it*, said I, *that I may haste to execute it.—I depend upon you*, answer'd she, *and hope you will be so much a Friend to yourself, as not to disappoint the good Opinion I have of you.—You must know there is a Lady of the highest Quality in* Venice, *who has taken a Disgust to a Woman, and would willingly have her dispatch'd into another World. She is at present in this House; but there are Reasons which made it not proper the Deed should be done here;—but early in the Morning,—I will put you in a Way.—*

The Horror which seiz'd my Soul at this monstrous Injunction, which by all Circumstances I was certain my Sister was the Contriver of, was too great for Description; but the Darkness (for it was Night) help'd me to conceal it from the Observation of this Wretch; and she bidding me be up by Break of Day, went into the House, leaving me to ruminate on what I had promis'd to perform. In the midst of my Concern for having a Sister oversway'd by her Passions to an Act so detestable, I rejoic'd that I had it in my Power to prevent the Perpetration of so black a Purpose, and spent the best Part of the Night in determining how I should contrive to preserve a Life, which I doubted not but her Malice would a second Time attempt, if she shou'd know she had been disappointed in the first. At last I bethought me of a Woman, who had formerly been a Nurse in our Family, and was now removed with her Husband to a little House a great Distance from any Town; there I resolved to secure the design'd Victim from any further Violence; and when I reflected on the Blessing this Chance would give me, I could scarce lament I had a Sister so cruel a Disposition, since to her Barbarity I should be indebted for a Joy, which 'twas probably not all my own Assiduity, and constant Services, would ever have been able to obtain.

As the unfortunate *Honorius* was in this Part of his Relation, the intermitting Torture which had given him liberty to utter thus much, return'd with treble Fury: He roar'd with Extremity of Anguish:—Nimble Twitches ran thro' all his Frame,—convulsing every Nerve:—Sure at that Time he must be possess'd with more than mortal Courage to sustain such Racks, else would he by some Act of Desperation have finish'd them at once.—

As *Myrtano* was going on in condoling the Misery this unhappy Gentleman had endur'd, *Idalia*, not a little amaz'd to hear that the unknown Person, to whom she was so much oblig'd, was *Honorius*, had the greatest Impatience imaginable to know the End of this Adventure; and that he might the sooner come to a Conclusion, desired he would wave all the Particulars in what Manner she had been preserv'd, and come to those of which she yet was ignorant.

Madam, *reply'd* Myrtano, he was not in a Capacity of relating much more than what I have recounted; there was in this last Fit so little Intermission of his Agonies, that he had only Space between them to run over, in as brief a Manner as he could, his Behaviour to you in the Forest, and his conducting you to the House he had thought of for you; but as he was just going to mention in what Part of the Country it stood, he was seiz'd with another Pain, which was to that Violence, that it entirely deprived him of his Senses, and from that Time all he said was so unconnect and wild, that nothing was to be inferred from it. I was infinitely troubled when I found it was not in his Power to give me any Account how he came, after he had left you, to my House again, to receive that fatal Drug from the Hands of *Ardella*; but resolving at my Return to force the Knowledge from her, I left my Servants, who by this Time were all come back, to attend the *Litter*, while I posted home to secure her. She, who was far from imagining what had reach'd my Ears, came into the Room immediately on my calling for her; and was beginning with a well-acted Disquiet to tell me a long Story of your making your Escape unknown to her; but I was too full of Distraction both for your being gone, and the dreadful Mischief which by her Means had fallen on *Honorius*, to endure to listen to her, and put a Stop to her Discourse by telling her I was made acquainted with her horrid Actions; and accusing her both with the Murder of you, and the very Man whom she had brib'd to that inhuman Deed, gave her so terrible a Fright, that she immediately fell on her Knees, and confess'd herself guilty. After which I oblig'd her to acquaint me with the Particulars of her Crime, and she recounted to me how, by the Instigations of Donna *Antonia*, she had given you a Letter, which was to make me appear guilty of the highest Baseness imaginable, and by the same cruel Woman's Orders had contriv'd your Death, and then that of the Person employ'd in it, fearing he might sometime or other betray what he had done: But when I told her, him whom she had poison'd was Don *Honorius*, the Brother of *Antonia*, and she saw him brought in, I thought the Creature would have dy'd with Fear: She again threw herself at my Feet, and trembling, conjur'd me to permit her to make her Escape; but I would not grant her Request, resolving, if *Honorius* dy'd, to give her up to Justice, and in the mean time had her confin'd in a Room on the Top of the House, when it was impossible for her to get away, without the Knowledge of the Servant whom I order'd to keep the Key: But by what Insinuations I know not, she beguil'd him to betray his Trust, and they both fled together; but where, I never could learn, nor indeed did I give myself much Trouble about it, knowing if the Business should come before a Magistrate, there would appear so much Intricacy in the Affair, especially when *Antonia* interpos'd her Cunning, as the Case for her own sake exceedingly required her to do, he would be extremely puzzled what Sentence to give. But to return to *Honorius*: When the Physician had examin'd his Pulse, and watch'd some Hours by him, and given proper Medicines to expel the Poison, he seem'd to be in great Hope of saving him. *Antonia*, whom I immediately writ to, with an Account of what had happen'd, came to *Vicenza*; almost as much distracted, or feign'd to be so, for the Mischief she had caus'd, as her Brother was. But not to spin out my Narration beyond your Patience, after a prodigious deal of lingering Torment, he at last was out of Danger, the Poison not happening to have been strong enough to seize the Seats of Life, tho' it miserably destroy'd the Outworks: He lost his Hair, Eyebrows, and the finest Set of Teeth that could be:—His Strength was very much decay'd, and all the Vivacity and Gaiety of his Temper was gone: Nothing of what he was remain'd, but his unextinguishable Passion for you; and that enabled him to take a Journey to the Place where he had left you, before he could get the Physician's Consent to venture a little Walk in the Garden; but contrary to all our Perswasions he went, tho' till his Return he made no Confident whither he was going, imagining, as he told me afterwards, that had I been appris'd of his Design, my Passion would have carry'd me there before him. And indeed he was not deceiv'd in his Conjecture; no Consideration should have withheld me a Moment, had I known what Place *Idalia's* Presence bless'd, and to that End watch'd every unguarded Word his Frenzy utter'd, in hope of discovering the dear Secret; but failing of it then, could not expect it at his Return of Reason. Never did I see a Man so oppress'd with Melancholy as he was, when he came back from seeking you: He then related to me where he had left you, and your Removal from thence, none knew to what Place; and lamented with so zealous a Concern the Improbability there was he ever should be so happy to see you more, that I, tho' his Rival, and brought into the same Misfortune by him, could not deny my Compassion to his Grief.—But why should I delay to tell you, that the Loss of you sat so near his Heart, that he grew weary of the World, resolv'd to appear in it no more, and enter'd into the Society of *Gray Friars*, of which there is a Convent at *Segonadica*. I was pretty near bearing him Company, for *Antonia* finding all the soft

Blandishments she made use of were ineffectual to work the End she aim'd at, made an Application to the *Doge*: The great Interest her Uncle the *Count* had with him, engag'd him to favour her Cause so far, as to leave me no other Choice than the Performance of my Contract with her, or go immediately into a Monastery, and by taking Orders set her at liberty to marry another. I will not trouble you with the Chagrin I was in at this arbitrary Decree, which yet I had no Appeal from.—You see me now her Husband.—Soon after I became so, Count *Miramont* died, and *Honorius* having forsook the World, the greatest Part of the vast Possessions he was master of fell to *Antonia*, on which Occasion we came to *Rome*, most of the Estate lying hereabouts: A Blessing, (*added he,*) little proportionable to that which Heaven has so unexpectedly favour'd me with, the meeting here the dear, the everlasting Mistress of my Soul, my never, never-to-be-forgotten *Idalia!*

He clos'd this long Discourse with a tender Pressure of her Hand, and such an Infinity of soft Transport in his Eyes, as sufficiently assur'd her Marriage had made no Alteration in his Sentiments. But she, who expected to hear something more of what the Designs of *Honorius* had been, ask'd *Myrtano*, if he had never heard any Mention of a Letter she had entrusted him with to her Father; which, after having begg'd her Pardon for omitting that Part of his Rival's Generosity, he inform'd her, that he told him, the Reason of his desiring her to write to Don *Bernardo*, was, that he might have a Pretence to wait on him, and declaring the Passion he long had for her, asked his Consent to make him happy; which if obtain'd, he would have return'd to her without his Disguise, and brought her back to *Venice* with an Equipage suitable to the Quality of Don *Bernardo's* Daughter and *Honorius's* Wife. *'Tis much,* (said *Idalia*), *that if he were possess'd of so sincere an Affection as what you represent, he discover'd not himself before he left me, having done me a Service which he might well believe would entitle him to my Esteem.—The Reason he gave me for it,* (answer'd *Myrtano* bowing,) *is such a one as is infinitely glorious to me; but I know not if you will pardon my repeating it.—He said, adorable* Idalia! *that he found you too full of Tenderness for the happy* Myrtano, *to hope he should be able to find Room in your Heart for any* second *Impression, till Time and Absence, and your Opinion of my Infidelity, had help'd him to eraze the* former. *Idalia* could not forbear blushing at these Words, which put her so much in mind of those she had utter'd in the Forest, little suspecting she had such a Witness of them. But she had a Person by her, who would not see her in that soft

Confusion without taking his Advantage of it, and making use of all those tender Artifices which Love inspires to charm the list'ning Fair, he at last won her to confess that he was still as dear to her as ever: He would not leave the Chamber till she had promis'd to stay with him for sometime, as at first she had made a Scruple of doing, since she imagin'd (as indeed it was natural enough to believe) *Antonia* would not only be excessively disquieted herself, but also contrive all the Means her Wit and Malice could furnish her with to render her so too. Nor did her Fears deceive her: Never was a Family more distracted than that of *Myrtano's*, the reliefs and indignant Temper of his Wife being, by his keeping a watchful Eye over all her Actions, prevented from bursting out in publick, she'd itself in the most trivial Concerns. She seem'd to make it her whole Study to disoblige him; and he on the other Side, heartily hating her, did all he could to break her Heart. The Servants were ever countermanded by the one, if about to do anything they were order'd by the other; *Myrtano* always exerting his Authority, would be obey'd, and *Antonia* was not of a Humour to endure it.—All their Days were pass'd in Quarrels, and their Nights in sullen Discontent.—*Idalia* alone was uncontroll'd, and free from those Jars with which the Ears of every other Person in the House were grated.—None presum'd to contradict her Will, and she had nothing to disturb her Repose, but what she endur'd from the Cause of so much Unhappiness to others. To make her Life more easy, the amorous *Myrtano* had prevail'd on her to throw off her Disguise of Men Cloaths, and in exchange for them had presented her with various Suits of the richest, and the most becoming a young Lady could wear; and to prevent the Servants, or any other Person who had seen her in another Garb, from making any Constructions to her Disadvantage on her Change of Habit, forc'd the haughty soul of *Antonia* to submit so far to his Humour, as to her own her still for a Relation of her's, who for some Reasons had for a Time thought fir to disguise her Sex.—What a Stab this must be to a Wife, let anyone judge!—But the Crimes she had been guilty of, in first conspiring against her Life, and afterwards in entertaining a Passion so contrary to her Matrimonial Vow, made it but just she should receive such Treatment: But as she was of a Nature too impatient to reflect on what she had done amiss, so she had also too much Pride to endure the Punishment without Agonies, which sometimes brought her into a Condition little differing from Madness.—She complain'd of her ill Fate, but had none to remedy it:—She curs'd, but had none to assist her in her Desire of Vengeance.—Fancy cannot form an *Idea* of more consummate Wretchedness than what this Lady suffer'd, compell'd to *obey*, yet eager to *command*,—wild to *proclaim* her Wrongs, yet oblig'd to call 'em *none*, lest by publishing her *Husband's* Faults, she should give him a Pretence for exposing *her's*.

*Idalia* all this while pass'd her Hours in those Amusements, in which her Soul most delighted; she list'ning to the incessant Vows, and soft Insinuations which daily fell from the enchanting Tongue of her ador'd *Myrtano*, rejoic'd to find him guilty of no other Infidelity than what his Fate compell'd him to; and transported that his Affections were rather heighten'd than diminish'd, and utterly forgetting the solemn Protestation she had made before she fled from *Vicenza*, never, on any Terms, to yield to see him more, or think of him but with Disdain and Hatred, a *Monastery* was now the least of her Desire; and tho' he had not yet offer'd at any Freedoms more than Innocence would allow, there was a small Probability that he would always continue to put so great a Constraint on his Inclinations;—yet did she either not consider it at all, or in so slight a Manner as gave her no Pain.—Those Apprehensions which had so much alarm'd her, when, to preserve her Honour, she hazarded all the Dangers of the Sea, were now no more:— Lull'd in the pleasing Lethargy of Love, Reflection slept, and all the vigorous Warnings of Virtue, Fame, and Reputation, were in the soft Enchantment hush'd to Peace:—She saw nothing but *Myrtano*;—heard nothing but *Myrtano*;—her Soul, all dissolv'd in tender Languishments, had no Leisure for any other Contemplation:—He soon perceiv'd it, and with soothing Art by unperceiv'd Degrees stole gently from one Liberty to another, till at last, almost unawares even to herself, she yielded to all his burning Passion aim'd at, and thought the guilty Joy sufficient Compensation for the Loss of Honour.

*Myrtano* had an unfashionable Constancy in his Nature, which made him not esteem *Idalia* the less for her giving him this last and greatest Proof of the Tenderness she had for him.—*Possession* was so far from *abating*, that it rather *increas'd* the Ardour of his Affections:—He never saw her without new Desires; each Look express'd unsatisfied Longings; and every Enjoyment was like the first, or more transporting. Thus for a Time were both as bles'd as the Gratification of their utmost Wishes could make them: But guilty Pleasures are never of any long Continuance; the inconsiderate Heart, which, quitting *Virtue*, places its whole Felicity in *Love*, sooner or *later*, must confess the Error, and curse in unavailing Penitence the luscious Crime which lured them on to Ruin. The Sense-enslav'd *Myrtano*, and his unthinking Mistress, were not permitted to riot many Months in their unlicensed Raptures, before as dreadful as unforeseen an Accident happen'd, which was the Occasion of separating them forever.

The enrag'd *Antonia* perceiving it an Impossibility ever to regain the Esteem of her Husband by the Measures she took, and disdaining to make us of any softer Means, bent her whole Thoughts on Vengeance:—The Contentment she saw in the Eyes both of him and *Idalia*, put her beyond all Patience;—she could not bear it;—and being, by *Myrtano's* Watchfulness, and Knowledge of her vindictive Nature, prevented from doing any Mischief to either of them, resolv'd to buy Revenge at any rate, she at last form'd a Design which she thought could not fail of answering her End.—What is it that Desperation is not capable of performing?—Those who value not their own Lives, with Ease may reach that of another's,—and *Death* to her was but a trivial Ill, in comparison with what she endur'd in Life;—she was willing to plunge into Perdition herself, provided she cou'd but drag the Persons she hated along with her. To facilitate her horrid Purpose, she affected to be much more satisfied in her Mind than of late she had been, and with an Air of Humiliation said to *Myrtano*, That being fully convinc'd that the Misfortune of estranging his Affections from her, had been wholly owing to her own ill Management, she was now struck with so sincere a Contrition for what she had done, that cou'd she but obtain a Pardon from him and *Idalia*, she would forsake the World, and retire to a Cloyster, and by her future Acts of Piety and Devotion, endeavour to expiate for the Errors of the past. He was too well acquainted with her Art of feigning, to depend much on the Truth of what she said, but wou'd not seem to question it, lest if she had really the Intentions she pretended, (as 'twas not impossible but she might,) his suspicion shou'd throw her into her former Violence of Temper, and occasion a Change in her Resolution, than the Execution of which nothing could have given him a greater Satisfaction. He communicated what had been told him, and his Sentiments of it to *Idalia*, who join'd in his Opinion, that there was scarce a Hope she shou'd in good earnest be so alter'd; and also that it was proper for 'em both, however, to counterfeit a Credulity, that, by seeming unguarded, they might the better penetrate into her Designs. But that requir'd more Skill than either of them were possess'd of: The subtil *Antonia* laid her Scheme too deep to be fathom'd by all their Artifices; she behav'd in such a Manner, that it was impossible not to believe her an entire Convert; she pray'd, fasted, wept, nay, really sent to the Convent of *Pour Clairs*, entreating they would accept of her; which being granted, and everything prepar'd for going, she begg'd that her Husband and *Idalia* wou'd pass an Hour or two in her Apartment, and accept a little Repast with her, before she took her everlasting Leave: She said she could not promise herself an entire Forgiveness of them, without they obliged her in this Request. Neither of them cou'd handsomely refuse her, tho' *Idalia* wou'd have been better pleased to have been excused; but the Consideration that it was the last Time she shou'd ever be shock'd with her Presence, made her the more easily comply.

A very noble Collation was provided; and *Antonia* still continuing to wear her Countenance of Mildness, taking up a large Silver Cup, which she had order'd to be fill'd with Wine.—*Here, Madam*, said she, *may all Offences between us be forever buried in Oblivion;—and you,* (pursu'd she, turning to *Myrtano,*) *my once lov'd* Husband, *and I hope my everlasting* Friend, *tho' in this World, Heaven and my own Misfortunes separate me from you, may we in another taste all those Joys which are denied me here:— Pledge me, both of you, or I shall think you have but half forgiven those Faults which Passion, Youth, and Inadvertency have made me guilty of.* Myrtano could not hear these Words, which were accompany'd with a Shower of well-dissembled Tears, without dissolving too; and now fully believing she was in earnest, cou'd not help pitying her Condition.—He took the Cup out of her Hand with a deep Sigh; but being about to drink, a Servant, who stood at the Door, observing all that past, ran hastily to him, and snatching from his Lips the fatal Draught, cry'd, *What is it you wou'd do, Signior? This Wine is Mingled with some pernicious Drug. What means the Fellow!* (interrupted he,) *dost thou not see* Antonia *has drank of it? But do not you,* (resum'd the other;) *I saw her when she believ'd no Eye but Heaven's was Witness of the Deed, take from her Pocket a little Viol full of something, which, I believe, was Poison, and pour it in that Cup, then call'd for Wine, and mingled them together. 'Tis false,* (cry'd *Antonia,*) *'tis false! and thou,* Myrtano, *hast suborn'd this Villain to accuse me, on purpose to make me hateful to the World, and rob me of that Compassion which my Sufferings merit.—Hold, Madam,* (said *Myrtano,* strangely amaz'd,) *moderate your Passion; if wrong'd, you shall have Justice. Tell me,* (continu'd he sternly, to the Fellow,) *by what Means came you to see this Action of your Lady, which you say she did with so much Privacy. I was coming into the Room,* (reply'd he, with an assur'd Accent,) *ignorant that anybody was in it, to fetch something I had forgot and left there when I had lighted up Candles: But as I was opening the Door, I saw my Lady, without being seen by her, for her Back was towards me; but standing opposite a great Glass and Candle by her, I had the Opportunity of discovering what she was about;—I plainly saw her mix the Liquors, which I should not have suspected to be Poison, had I not also heard her speak to herself these Words,*—Revenge is more than Life; *and presently after,* I cannot feel the Pains of Hell, while I see them in 'em; *(said she,)* Damnation will be Pleasure, if they share it with me. *This,* Signior, (continu'd he, bowing,) *was sufficient to make me fear she had something more in Agitation than she pretended, and oblig'd me to watch to whom that Cup was offer'd. Oh! 'tis all a monstrous Lye,* (interrupted she;) *you see he contradicts himself: He says 'tis Poison, and that he watch'd to whom I offer'd it:—Did I not myself first drink, and would I destroy myself?—I know not* (said *Myrtano*) *to what Extremes you may have had recourse; but if you have here mix'd any Ingredients unfit for me to take,—thus I disappoint your Aim.* With these Words he took the Cup out of the Fellow's Hand, and dash'd all that was in it on the Floor. This Action made *Antonia* throw off the mask of meek Humility, and appear the Fury: *But I will not be disappointed,* cried she, snatching a Sword which by Accident lay on the Window, and running at *Idalia, nor Heaven nor Earth shall ward my Vengeance here.* But she soon found herself mistaken; *Myrtano* was quick enough to wrest the Weapon from her, with these Words, *Vile Woman,* said he, *now you appear yourself; but as the shameful Passion you had for this Lady, while you believed her in a Capacity of returning it, preserved her once from my mistaken Rage; so shall my Care both now and ever shield her from your Malice. And must I then die alone* (cried she in a distracted Tone,) *must all I have done serve but to leave you free for the Embraces of a Rival?—And must she, that hated Cause of all my Misery, be blest when I am no more?—O torment, worse than Hell!—Snatch,—snatch me, Fiends, there's not a Spirit damn'd among you feels half my Pains!—Yes, I confess I would have poisoned both; and 'twas the only Joy Thought could allow my lost forlorn Condition, that I should see you, cursing each other in the Pangs of Death for those hot Wishes which brought on your Ruin;—then sink together to the lowest Hell, where I should follow, and be your Tormentor still.—Oh!* (continued she, endeavouring to fly at *Idalia,*) *that vile Enchantress, whose bewitching Smiles first taught my Soul to know an unchaste Desire, had she but perished with me, I would have absolved my Fate of all Injustice.*

In this manner did she rave, till Don *Myrtano*, thinking what was most proper to be done, after having took the trembling *Idalia* out of the Room, sent for Physicians to endeavour, if possible, to expel the envenom'd Draught before it had operated too far. But they soon found she had not drank a sufficient Quantity to endanger Life, tho' it happen'd not thro' Care, having no other Design than to die with those her Revenge was so zealous to send out of the World; knowing the very Manner of their Deaths cou'd not be kept a Secret, and that Law wou'd not suffer such Murders to go unpunish'd. In spite of the Impatience of her Temper, which, longer than else it wou'd have been, protracted her Recovery, she was perfectly well in a few Days. But this Adventure being whisper'd about from one to the other, (as in such a Family it could not be otherwise,) made so great a Noise in *Rome*, that it came at last to the Ears of his *Holiness*: He had a particular Regard for *Myrtano*, on the Account of his good Qualities; and for *Antonia*, as she was Niece to Count *Miramont*, for whom he had had a very great Friendship; and being concern'd to hear of so unhappy a Disturbance between them, sent for them to know the Truth of the Affair. *Myrtano* wou'd have gloss'd it over in as plausible a Manner as he cou'd; but his enrag'd Wife, whose Fury was not in the least abated, rejoic'd in this Opportunity of exposing him and *Idalia*; which she did in the most bitter and in invective Terms her Malice cou'd invent: And this Proceeding oblig'd him, in return, to lay open all her Actions, her Intention to murder that Lady while at *Vicenza*, the base Contrivance of the Letter which drove her from that Place, the Poison which *Ardella*, by her Orders, gave the *unknown* Person, who proved to be her Brother Don *Honorius dell Miramont*; her Passion for *Idalia* while she believ'd her to be a Man; and lastly, her Design of poisoning both him and her. So monstrous a Catalogue of Vices turn'd the Holy Examiner entirely against her; he cou'd no longer endeavour to perswade them to a Reconciliation, and told *Antonia* she was a Woman of too dangerous a Disposition to be left at her own Liberty, and therefore order'd she should be forthwith confin'd for Life in that very Convent of *Pour Clairs*, which she had pretended to go to out of Devotion. As for *Myrtano*, he chid him a little for giving Cause of Provocation, and told him he must resolve to part with *Idalia*, it being consistent with neither of their Reputations to live together; and that it was not only the Ruin of the Souls to continue in that Course of Life, but also of *Antonia's*, who would never be a thorough Convert till she was eased of the Torments of Jealousy. He closed the pious Exhortations he had made as a *Priest*, with a positive Command as *Pope* and supreme Dictator, that *Idalia* should quit his House immediately, and from that Moment he should refrain her Company. This last Sentence afforded some Contentment to the restless state of *Antonia*, and she obey'd her own with less Reluctance, as sensible they wou'd not be less miserable in being separated from each other, than she was in the Disappointment of the Revenge she purposed.

But what Tongue is able to express the Despair the poor *Idalia* fell into, when *Myrtano* brought her home these doleful Tidings? At first he had Power only to inform her with his Eyes that he had something fatal to unfold; but the dreadful Secret must be told, and bursting Sights, half Words, and broken Sentences, at last made her know the worst:—She wept, swoon'd, almost dy'd away, while he was speaking: Nor were his Agonies inferior to those which she endured. But there was no resisting a Power, such as that which had decreed their Misfortune, at least while they continued at *Rome*:—All that remained to prop up falling Hope, was a Promise he made her of removing as soon as he could dispose of what Effects he had here, either out of the *Pope's* Dominions, or to some remote Part of then, whence no Intelligence of their Behaviour might reach his Knowledge. This comforted her a little, and she went to a House where he had provided her a Lodging, and Servants to attend her. It happen'd to be in a very pleasant Part of the City, next Door to a Monastery of *Benedictines*, among whom a great number of Ladies of the best families in *Rome*, he hoped, by being acquainted with them, and visiting there sometimes, she might find some Alleviation to her Sorrows. It was sometime before she could bring herself even to wish to receive any Consolation; but being by his daily Importunities (for he constantly writ her) prevailed on to divert herself by all Means that were in her Power, she one Day took a little Walk in the Cloyster-Gardens: While she was there, the Bell rung, and having a little Curiosity to see the Nuns at Prayers, when into the Chapel, where almost the first she cast her Eyes on was a Face perfectly known to her, tho' she could not presently recollect where she had seen in; but going a little nearer, she soon knew the Lady to be the beautiful *Bellraizia*, who, she thought, had perished in the Storm from which herself had so narrowly escaped. The high Esteem she had conceived for her, made her extremely glad to see her safe, but the finding her in that Society, so contrary to the Religion she had been educated in, and her Engagements with *Abdomar*, gave her an adequate Concern, not doubting but that unhappy Gentleman was lost. She longed impatiently for the End of the Ceremony, that she might be informed what had occasioned so strange an Alteration; and singling herself from the Crowd, and standing in a Corner of the Chapel, as near as she could to that Place where the Nuns go out, she gave her a little pluck by the Sleeve as she passed by; which the fair *Nun* perceiving, made a Stop, and looking on *Idalia*, immediately knew her. There passed several Congratulations between them for their mutual Deliverance from so imminent a Danger; but the Place they were in not allowing any long Conversation, *Idalia* could be made acquainted with no more at that Time than that *Abdomar* had also been preserved; and the being told this, was no small Addition to the Surprise she had been in before; which the beautiful *Convert* easily discerning, told her with a Smile the Wonder should be satisfied, if she would favour her with a Visit the next Day; which *Idalia* assuring that she would, took her Leave.

At the Time appointed she enquired for her at the Grate, where a Couple of young *Devotees* where standing, and was answered by one of them, That as for *Bellraizia*, they knew nothing of her by that Name, but that a Lady of a foreign Nation had lately enter'd herself among them, which 'twas probably was the same she enquired for, for she had been but lately christen'd, and was called *Theresa*. *Idalia* imagining it might be she, desired to see her, and the other very obligingly ran to fetch her, who was indeed the same. After a little Discourse in ordinary Affairs, *Idalia* expressing her Impatience to know what had been the Occasion this sudden Turn in her Principles, as well as Affairs, entreated she would give a Solution to what at present appear'd so great a Riddle: *I must be more rude and unpolite than the most Ignorant of the Country I came from,* (answered the lovely Proselyte,) *if I should refuse to satisfy a Demand which so obligingly testifies you take some little Interest in my Concerns, and have not forgot the Friendship we promised to each other, at a Time when neither of us expected to meet in any other Place than that which we then were in. But because to relate only what has befallen me since I had the Happiness of seeing you, would render the History of my Life imperfect, if you please I will run over, with as much Brevity as the several Incidents will permit, the Remainder of those Misfortunes, which the Tempest oblig'd me to break off.* *Idalia* thanking her with a low Bow for the Trouble she was about to give herself, sat down to listen to what she said, which was in this Manner:

*The Continuance of the History of* Abdomar *and* Bellraizia.

ELIZA HAYWOOD

I Was confined (*said she*) in the Manner I told you for several Days before I saw any Person from whom I could learn any News how *Abdomar* had been disposed of; which gave me a Rack of Thought infinitely superior to what I felt on my own Account. The first that visited me was *Zatilda*, enjoined by her Father, and mine, and *Mulyzeden*, (as she did not fail of letting me know,) to dive into my Sentiments, and find out if possible the Truth of the whole Affair between me and *Abdomar*: Because of the Posture he had been found in by the *Prince*, made them all positive that I had been made acquainted with his Passion. And nothing, she told me, could convince them that I had not only listen'd to, but also allow'd of his Courtship, if I did not instantly consent to ratify the Contract with *Mulyzeden*. You may believe 'twas with an inexpressible Trouble she brought me these Tidings, not doubting but that I should be obliged to comply, to the eternal Ruin of her Hopes: But I assured her to the contrary by all the Asservations I could make, protesting I would rather die than make her so unhappy, if no other Obstacle but my Friendship to her had interpos'd; but as I loved the Charming *Abdomar*, and was beloved by him with an equal Height of Passion, though his Generosity obliged him to conceal it from me, no Threats, no Tortures, should force me to act so contrary both to my own Wishes and theirs, who of all the World were dearest to me. My renewing the Vows I had before made her on this Score, dissipated great Part of the Chagrin she brought with her; but, alas! she had it not in her Power to give any Relief to mine, having been able to learn nothing concerning *Abdomar*, but that he was in close Prison, and that *Mulyzeden* was yet irresolute what Sentence to pass on him. All the dreadful Examples of which I had heard or read of jealous Love, came into my Head the Moment she told me this: I fancied I saw him bleeding, dying, for my sake, and begged *Zatilda* for her own sake (since nothing else could give her the Happiness she wished) and for the sake of us all to permit me to reveal the Secret of her Passion for *Mulyzeden: That* (said I) *once known, will oblige the* King *not to take it ill that I refused to do, what done, would make his Daughter wretched.— My Father will not dare to force my Inclinations against the Interest of his Princess, and* Mulyzeden *cannot but glory in the Exchange.—All of us may be happy in our several Wishes, would you consent.*—But all I could urge was in vain to win this modest Princess to give me the Liberty I ask'd; she swore rather to die than proffer Love; and we parted without being able to resolve on anything for our common Satisfaction.

It must be only the Imagination of a Person involved in the same Perplexities I was; can figure an *Idea* of what I endured in the Reflection of my unhappy State; but as I was sitting alone, after *Zatilda* had left me, the Windows being open for Coolness, I saw something fly in at one of them, and fall at my Feet: Stooping to take it up, I perceived it was a Paper; which hastily opening, I found it contain'd these Lines, which I too often repeated to forget, and were in this Manner.

To the Divine Bellraizia

*I* Believe it needless to inform you, that the Posture I was found in by my Prince, has occasion'd a Jealousy of me: But I confess I have not Generosity enough to suffer so great a Misfortune as the Loss of his Friendship without wishing to be pity'd by her, for whom I am content to endure greater Ills. *Mulyzeden* accuses me, most excellent Princess, of adoring you; and, oh! I acknowledge the involuntary Crime! But as my Lips have ne'er offended by any presumptious Declarations, I hope, though he cannot, Goodness, like your's, will pardon a Transgression, which I doubt not but I have as many Sharers in, as there are Souls to be sensible of your Perfections. I am but this Moment released from my Confinement, and in a few Hours must leave *Barbary* forever. All I entreat for myself, is your Forgiveness; and that you will believe the Crime for which I am banished, I never should have had the Boldness to reveal, had I not been assured you would have known it without me.

My *next* Request, is, that you will do that justice to my Prince, which his unbounded Passion, and a Million of excellent Qualifications, make him merit: And my *last* to the Gods, that the choicest Blessings in their Power to give, may ever be the Portion of you both, whatever is decreed for entreating your Blessing, and avowing myself ever

The Unhappy Abdomar

In what Manner shall I make you sensible of the tender Languishments which at the reading this took up my Soul?—But 'twas not long that soft Confusion lasted; the Reflection that he was going, that I should never see him more, embittered all the Sweets which the Contemplation of so generous a Passion had afforded.—But why should I detain you with the particular Emotions which agitated me according as the different Thoughts rose in me:—In fine, I lov'd, and could not bear to lose him.—All the Remonstrances of Honour, Grandeur, Reputation, were silenced by the more powerful Calls of Love: Since he was banished, I resolved to be the Partner of his Exile, whatever should ensue.—You'll say, considering the Circumstance I then was in, this was a Resolution which promis'd little Facility in the Execution; yet difficult as it was, the Passion which prompted it, inspired me also with a Contrivance to perform it: I bribed one of my Women to procure me a Suit of Clothes, such as our *Negro* Slaves are wont to wear; and oiling my Face, and afterwards rubbing it over with some Powder, made of the Shells of Chestnuts, and tying up my Hair close to my Head, and covering it with a little Taffety Cap, made myself appear so like one of those I designed to pass for, that I had not the least Fear of being suspected. I also prevailed on the same Woman, whom I had made my Confident, to put on my Clothes; and if any Person from the *King*, Prince *Mulyzeden*, of my Father, should happen to be sent soon after I was gone, to lie down on the Bed, feigning an Indisposition, that they might not discover it was any other than myself that spoke; and exacted a solemn Vow from her, that whatever happened, she should not confess she knew anything of my Escape to any other Person but *Zatilda*. Everything answered my Wish; *Abdomar* having Leave till the next Morning to prepare for his Journey, I mingled with his Train, and found Means to be entertained among them. I now thought myself most happy, so easily can Love answer for the want of all Things else; not that I was so abandoned to Modesty as to discover myself to him I had run such Risques to follow; no, I proposed no other Satisfaction in this Flight than to avoid *Mulyzeden*, and enjoy the Presence of the Man I loved; and, indeed, it was a Felicity unconceivable that I took in thus, unknown by him, observing all his Motions, in which I found nothing but what served more to encrease my Admiration and Esteem.

But, alas! this Scene of innocent Delight met with a sudden Interruption: We had not travelled above fifty Miles from the Court of *Barbary*, before we were overtaken, and seiz'd by a Party of the King's Horse sent after in pursuit of us. *Abdomar* demanding the Reason, was answered by the Captain, That he must bring back the Princess *Bellraizia*, or discover where she was, since she had made her Escape, and 'twas believed by his Instigation.—*Abdomar* express'd the highest Concern, as well as Astonishment, at hearing this; but protested, as very well he might, that he was entirely innocent of it. But this could not serve his Turn; the Captain was obliged to obey Orders, and we were all brought back; and *Abdomar* was immediately conducted into the Council-Chamber, where all that had Interest in it were assembled to examine him concerning me.—The Horrors I endured while this lasted, were such as it would be impossible to describe: I imagined that his Innocence would stand him in but little stead to defend him against a Party, who were resolved to think him guilty; nor was I mistaken, they disbelieving all he said, and imagining that if I were not really in his Company, it was on his Account I had left *Barbary*, and that there was some Place agreed on for our Meeting, ordered he should be rack'd to make him confess. This Doom being pass'd, he was brought out; and the Sight of those Men by him, whom I knew to be the common Executioners of those kind of Torments, made me know to what he was decreed; and wild with the Horror of his suffering them on any Account, much more on mine, I lost all Sense either of Shame or Danger to myself, and running in amongst the Guards, cried out to them, *And is it for the Princess* Bellraizia *that the noble* Abdomar *must endure the Rack?—If so, let him be remanded back; I can produce the Princess, and clear his Innocence.* Everybody that stood near enough to hear me, were strangely alarm'd at what I said, and some of them, running to the Council-Chamber, inform'd the *King* of what I said; on which the Torments decreed for *Abdomar* were suspended, and myself and he introduc'd.

You may believe how great a Damp 'twas to me, when I say the *King*, my Father, *Mulyzaden*, and all the Prime of the nobility, before whom I must either discover what I had done, and the Reasons which occasioned it, to suffer the whole Weight of their Indignation to fall on him who was infinitely dearer to me than either Life or Honour. Therefore being demanded what I had to offer in the Defence of *Abdomar*, and what I knew of *Bellraizia*, I boldly answered what they asked with another Question, which was, That if I proved the Prince's Flight unknown to *Abdomar*, whether they had any other Crimes to accuse him of? And all of them assuring me, that if I did so he was entirely at his Liberty, nothing farther having been alledged against him, I pull'd off my Cap, and letting my Hair fall about my Shoulders, *See here then*, (said I, with a Courage which I have been since supris'd at myself,) *see here that* Bellraizia *whom you seek, and whom nothing but the Guilt of permitting an innocent Person to suffer for a Crime she alone is guilty of, should have obliged to have discovered herself either to you, or any other.* The Amazement of the whole Assembly was in, gave me leave to make a farther Explanation of my Meaning, and I recounted to them the Aversion I had for *Mulyzeden*, my Passion for *Abdomar* even before I had the least Hope he would return it, and, in fine, the whole Truth of my Proceedings, bating what concern'd *Zatilda*: And indeed it had happened much better, if I had also discovered that; but she had bound me in so strict a Promise, that I durst not break through it without her Consent. To give you a Description of the different Agitations which I saw in the Countenances of the three I had most Reason to observe, the *King*, my Father, and the Prince, would be too tedious, so I shall only say, the Fury which I saw in one, could be equall'd only by the others: All were alike incens'd, tho' for contrary Reasons.

I Could not be a judge in what Manner *Abdomar* heard so unexpected a Discovery, both because he stood a little behind me, and also that Shame would have prevented me from looking on him with that Earnestness which I did on the other: But if one may form a Judgment by the Passion he has since prov'd he was inspired with, his Emotions must at that Time be more than ordinary. But to return to my Relation; My Father was the first that broke Silence, and looking on me with an Eye that sparkled with Indignation, *It is not* (said he) *this shameful accusing of yourself, that ought to skreen that Traytor from the Hands of Justice?—Yes*, (interrupted *Mulyzeden* no less fiercely,) *'tis plain he is guilty; for tho' the Princess has so ingloriously condescended to yield to his Desires, I never can believe she would be brought to it without Professions, such as she thought merited her Compassion. 'Tis false*, (resum'd I, enraged that all I could do was like to be ineffectual,) *and thou, unbelieving Prince, deservest not to be bless'd with such a Friend as* Abdomar. Then I pluck'd out of my Pocket a Letter he had thrown in at my Window, which was a sufficient Testimony that he never had so much as declared his Passion for me, much less had importuned me to go with him, to back what I said. The Princess *Zatilda*, who hearing what had pass'd the first Time that *Abdomar* had been examin'd in the Council, and well knowing he had no Share in my Flight, stepp'd into the Room to clear him of this Charge, and immediately knowing me, vouch'd the Truth of what I had alledged. All these Witnesses inclin'd the King, who was a perfect Lover of Justice, however prejudicial it might be to his Interest, to recall the Sentence he had pass'd on *Abdomar*; at which *Mulyzeden*, whose

Rage was nothing abated by the Knowledge that what I had done, had proceeded only from my own inconsiderate Passion, and thinking himself affronted on all Sides, turning to the King, *Your Majesty,* said he, *may, whenever you please, revoke your own Decrees, but neither Heaven nor Earth shall debar me from the Prosecution of mine:—I have vow'd the Traytor's Death, and thus I make it good.* In speaking these Words, he ran at *Abdomar* with all the Fierceness of an inveterate Malice; but that injur'd Gentleman did not now, as he had done before, bow to receive the Wound he offer'd, but snatching a Sword from a Lord that stood near him, put himself in an Posture of Defence as soon as he perceived the Prince's Design: *Time was,* (said he,) *I wou'd have welcom'd Death, but now have Cause to value Life, and must, and will defend it for the divine* Bellraizia, *tho' against you, next to her, dearest to my Soul.—Villain, thou liest,* (resum'd the Prince,) *nor shall thy Flattery move me to Forgiveness.* The Guards, which waited at the Door, were call'd in immediately, and having parted them, by the King's Command, bore *Abdomar* to the same Prison he had been in before; not that he was to be treated any longer as a Criminal, but his Majesty thought it most convenient for his Safety, to secure him there from the Fury of *Mulyzeden.* He made me a low Reverence, with such an inexpressible Tenderness in his Eyes, so soft an Extasy for what I had declared, as was beyond what any Words could have acknowledg'd; but I, tho' I observ'd it with as much Rapture as my Circumstances would allow, was in too much confusion to make any Return to the endearing Charm: But when he was gone, and I was left alone to the Upbraidings of the whole Assembly, (for there was not one there who did not blame my Conduct,) what did I not endure! None but *Zatilda* took my Part, and endeavour'd to excuse my Proceedings, by pleading the Force of that unconquerable Passion which had been the Cause of them; but she was immediately silenced by her Father, asking her how she came to be so well acquainted with Emotions so contrary to Reason, and to Honour: But Prince *Mulyzeden*, who still loved me, entreated them to cease any further Reproaches, and told me, That if I would permit him to espouse my Cause, by giving him that Happiness my Vows had long since made his Due, all I had done for *Abdomar* should be forgot. *No, Sir,* (said I,) *I have not gone so far in the Race of Passion to go back:—I own your Generosity, but 'tis* Abdomar *alone I can love.*—As I was proceeding, my Father interrupted me, crying out, *Degenerate Girl! unworldly the Regard of this noble Prince?—But in the Punishment I will inflict on thee, he shall perceive how I resent the Indignity thou hast offer'd him.—Here,* (continu'd he, to some of the Guards,) *bear her to her Appartment, and let her be shifted of these dishonourable Rags;—these shameful Witnesses of her Folly.* The Princess *Zatilda* had leave to accompany me, but had it not in her Power to give me much Consolation, or to receive it herself; and I believe never two had more Distraction in their Thoughts than we.—I again endeavour'd, by all the Arguments I was Mistress of, to perswade her to permit me to reveal the kind Thoughts she had of *Mulyzeden*; but she was still obstinate, and would listen to nothing I could say on that Score, and conjured me afresh never to let the Secret slip. But Providence brought it to light without my Breach of Promise; and we might all have been happy, if Modesty, which in others is the greatest Virtue, had not, by its Excess, been her Enemy, and disappointed the Aim of Heaven: One of my Women, who, it seems, had been appointed to attend me only as a Spy, listen'd to the Conversation we had together, and related it to both out Fathers; which you may guess as no small Surprise to them: But mine was so much vex'd at it, as believing this would certainly take away all Hope of my ever being Princess of *Fez*, that crossing his Ambition, he fell into a Fever, of which he dy'd. The King set me at liberty immediately after his Death, but would not disoblige the Prince so much as to give me leave to marry *Abdomar*, who was still in confinement.—*Zatilda* was yet ignorant that her Secret had been discover'd and the *King* perceiving that *Mulyzeden* still had the same Passion for me as ever, knew not which way to bring it about; but at last, finding his Daughter grow extremely ill, (as that poor Princess had ever since been consuming with inward Agonies,) he proposed the Matter to him. Never Man had a greater Share of Generosity than that unhappy Prince; and he could not hear he was beloved by a Princess, whom it was not his Destiny to love, without an Infinity of Concern, but had nothing of those Sentiments, which were requisite to make her happy. However, the tender Concern which fill'd his Soul, might possibly have ripen'd into something more to her Advantage, had she not put herself past the Power of receiving it: The Discourse the King had with him on this Score, was in the Palace-Garden, in that very *Grotto* where I had made the Discovery of the Passion which *Abdomar* had for me: The ill-fated *Zatilda* happen'd to be in one Part of it, while they were in the other, and over-heard all that pass'd; and overcome with Shame that the Secret was discover'd, and guessing by the Answers which *Mulyzeden* made, that she was like to receive no other Benefit by it than the Compassion of the Man she loved, resolved to put an End to the Miseries she had endured, and full of Desperation, plung'd that Moment a Dagger into her Breast. The Noise which her Fall made among the Trees and twisted Branches, of which the *Grotto* was composed, obliged her Father, and the Person for whose sake she had done this, to rise from their Seats, and look what 'twas occasion'd it.—It would be needless to repeat the Lamentations of a most tenderly loving Father, to find his only Child welt'ring in her Blood, and breathing her last; or those which *Mulyzeden* made, when he reflected he had been the Cause, tho' an innocent one: You may easily imagine they were suitable to the Occasion, and to the Characters of the Persons concern'd it. The most eminent Surgeons were send for; but the fatal Weapon had reach'd too far, and she lived no longer than to receive some Words of Compassion from him, who tho' he could not love, protested after he would gladly have exchanged Conditions, and bought the Preservation of her Life at the Expence of his own.

When she was gone, there was nothing in the Coast of *Barbary* which could induce me to stay in it: And having obtain'd Leave, I retired into the Country, to a Castle which had been my Father's. *Mulyzeden* would not offer to oppose it, nor had made any Visits to me since the Death of *Zatilda*, because he would give no Umbrage to the *King*; and I hop'd my absenting myself, fully convincing him that I never would be his, would oblige him to return to *Fez*, or at least to set *Abdomar* at liberty, who, I was confident, as soon as he was so, would find some Means to let me know it. But, alas! that too constant Prince could not forget his Passion! all my Unkindness had not the Power of effacing my Idea in his Soul! he continu'd to love me with an Ardency which was unvanquishable but by Death, which at last he yielded to! And sure if anyone ever had a broken Heart, he had, for he died of no other Disease but Grief. I have often wonder'd, that, considering the Sweetness of his Disposition, he had all this while kept *Abdomar* in Custody; but Jealousy and disappointed Love can know no Medium in their Rage. The Moment he was dead, the King gave Orders that he should be discharg'd, but desir'd he never would be seen in *Barbary*. I had an immediate account of all Things, and met him in the Way. After a thousand mutual Demonstrations of the tenderest Affection, we exchang'd Vows never to be parted more; and neither *Barbary* nor *Fez* promising much Security, he bethought him of buying a Ship, and living a Rover on the Sea, that being a Province where no mortal Prince had Power to drive us from. We had been eight

ELIZA HAYWOOD

Months without ever setting our Feet on Land, when that dreadful Storm, in which we thought you lost, shew'd us that Heaven deny'd its Approbation of our Love. However, it prevail'd not to separate us: Clasp'd in each other's Arms, we resolv'd, since there was no Hope of living, to die together. But when we thought ourselves most in danger, we were most secure; that Part of the Ship in which we were, was that which was dash'd against the Rock, and the other being rent forcibly away, this seem'd fasten'd to it, and the Storm immediately ceasing, we remain'd in our tatter'd Castle, till some Boats coming to our Relief, carry'd us safe on Shore.

In the House we were directed to, there was a Friar, certainly the most holy of his Order: Being inform'd of Part of our Story by *Abdomar* and myself, he told me very freely, that the Breach of my Vows to *Mulyzeden* had drawn the Vengeance of Heaven on me; and then began to argue with so divine a Zeal on the mistaken Precepts of our Religion, that in a few Days he won us both to embrace the Christian Faith, which my Ancestors had so shamefully abjur'd. To expiate the Sin of living so long in a State of Infidelity, he told us it was necessary to do something more than a bare Acknowledgment we had been in an Error; and in fine, in spite of the unbated Passion we still had for each other, he wrought on us both so far as to prevail on us to take Orders: And by mortifying our Desires in the tenderest Part, endeavour to appease the Offences we had been guilty of. *Abdomar*, as well as myself, submitted to it, and he is now with this good Friar among the *Capuchins*, and I am settled here, where so unexpectedly I have had the good Fortune to meet a Person in whose Conversation I promise myself much Comfort.

The charming *Convert* here finish'd her Narration; and *Idalia* reflecting on the Instability of that Felicity which only Love bestows, began to grow exceeding melancholy; which the other observing, entreated to know the Cause, and also what had befallen her since their Separation; which she complying with, let the new-made Christian know, that there were both Misfortunes and Inadvertencies occasion'd by Passion, as great as what she had experienc'd.

The visiting this Lady was all the Consolation *Idalia* had in her Separation from *Myrtano*; but she being soon after taken ill of so malignant a Fever, that it was thought dangerous to approach her, she not only lost the Company of one whose Wit and good Humour often diverted her from any despairing Thoughts, to which of late she was too liable, but also of one whose Strictness to the Principles she had embrac'd, might in Time have won her to a Belief, that true Happiness was only to be found in Virtue. And indeed in the Circumstance she then was, never Woman stood more in need of an Adviser: The living in the Manner she had done with *Myrtano*, his Wife's Desperation, and the *Pope's* decree, had made too great a Noise in *Rome* not to make her be publickly remark'd; and embolden'd by the Knowledge that she had been a *Mistress*, brought all the young and gay Part of the Town to sollicite for the same Favour; nay, some of them used so little Ceremony as to make her acquainted with their Designs on the first Visit, and others, treating her as a *Courtezan*, demanded to know her Price. Some would agree with her for a Month, others for a Week; all the Insults that Women of that Possession are liable to, she met with; which, considering that Haughtiness of her Disposition, could not be expected but to drive her to Extreams. She writ daily to *Myrtano*, conjuring him to made what Expedition he could to leave *Rome*; and he continu'd to assure her, he was as impatient as herself. But Things not being ready to lay violent Hands on her own Life, rather than endure them longer: She began to curse the Cause which had reduc'd her to a Condition, such as could give room for Liberties so contrary to what she had been us'd to receive, and could so ill bear:—She wanted Revenge on all who durst to use her in this Manner;—and not having it in her Power, was ready to burst with inward Spleen, and stifled Indignation. In this enrag'd Temper, happening to look out of her Window, she saw a young *Chevalier* pass by, whom imagining she had seen before, she look'd more earnestly at, and soon discover'd it to be *Florez*, the Villain who had first betray'd her from her Father's House, and been the Cause of all her Woe. A sudden Thought came into her Head at Sight of him: To be reveng'd on him for all, she sent a Servant after immediately, to watch where he went; which being inform'd of, she sat down, and disguising her Hand as much as possible, writ to him in this Manner:

## To Don FLOREZ

A chevalier, so accomplish'd as you, cannot be surpris'd to be told the Impression you have made on a Heart who pretends to a Capacity of distinguishing.—but I will not go about to tell you how much I am influenc'd by your Perfections, till I see how you approve the Conquest you have made over me: if

ELIZA HAYWOOD

you have an Hour to spare, bestow it this Evening in the long
Walk behind the *Benedictine* Nunnery, and just about the close
of day you shall meet

*Your enamour'd*
INCOGNITA

She did not doubt but the Vanity of his Disposition would make
him swallow the Bait she had prepar'd for him, and sent it by a Servant,
charging him not to discover either her Name, or where she lived, if
*Florez* should enquire, as 'twas probable he *would*. But the Fellow, who
was hired by *Myrtano* to attend her, and knew very well it was to him
she was indebted for a Support, thought it a monstrous Infidelity to his
Lord; and instead of delivering it to *Florez*, carry'd it directly to him.
The Astonishment with which he read it, is not to be express'd; but
resolving to inform himself to what Lengths the Perfidy he imagined
her guilty of would carry her, he muffled himself up in his Cloak, and
went himself at the appointed Time to the Place of Assignation, where
he had not waited long before he perceiv'd her coming. There was so
little Difference in their Stature, that she might be easily deceiv'd; and
coming near him, *I believe, Signior,* (said she,) *you are the Person I would
speak with: Are you not call'd Don* Florez? *I am,* (reply'd *Myrtano,* in a low
and feign'd Voice) *You had a Letter,* (resum'd she, drawing a Dagger, and
striking it with all her Force into his Breath, before he had Opportunity
to discover who he was,) *and now I give a Present such as your Villany
deserves.* She had Opportunity to say no more, he falling, immediately
cry'd out, O Idalia! *what have you done?*—These Words, the Voice, and
a closer Observation, made her know to whom she had given the Blow;
but all that can be conceiv'd of distracting Grief, of Horror without a
Name, was short of what she felt at this amasing Sight: She tore her
Hair and Face, rav'd, stamp'd, curs'd Fate, and scarce spar'd Heaven
in the Extremity of her Anguish: She threw herself upon his bleeding
Body, and kiss'd a thousand Times the Wound she had made.—But
this affording but little Satisfaction to the Racks of Thought, which
at this shocking Moment hurry'd her wild Brain, she started up, and
snatching the dagger, plung'd it thro' her Heart. He had just Power
to open his Eyes, and see the dreadful Reparation she had made him,
and then clos'd them forever. She lived some Hours to relate what she
had done, and the Cause that moved her to it, to some Persons whom
the Exclamations she made drew thither; but not long enough to see

the Justice of Heaven executed on *Florez*, who being fled from *Venice* for a Murder he had been guilty of, was discover'd at *Rome*, and there apprehended, and on the Account of many other base Actions, wholly friendless, he suffer'd the Law, and dy'd as much unpity'd, as *Myrtano* and his unfortunate Mistress were the contrary.

FINIS

# A Note About the Author

Eliza Haywood (1693–1756) was an English novelist, poet, playwright, actress, and publisher. Notoriously private, Haywood is a major figure in English literature about whom little is known for certain. Scholars believe she was born Eliza Fowler in Shropshire or London, but are unclear on the socioeconomic status of her family. She first appears in the public record in 1715, when she performed in an adaptation of Shakespeare's *Timon of Athens* in Dublin. Famously portrayed as a woman of ill-repute in Alexander Pope's *Dunciad* (1743), it is believed that Haywood had been deserted by her husband to raise their children alone. Pope's account is likely to have come from poet Richard Savage, with whom Haywood was friends for several years beginning in 1719 before their falling out. This period coincided with the publication of *Love in Excess* (1719–1720), Haywood's first and best-known novel. Alongside Delarivier Manley and Aphra Behn, Haywood was considered one of the leading romance writers of her time. Haywood's novels, such as *Idalia: Or, The Unfortunate Mistress* (1723) and *The Distress'd Orphan; or Love in a Madhouse* (1726), often explore the domination and oppression of women by men. *The History of Miss Betsy Thoughtless* (1751), one of Haywood's final novels, is a powerful story of a woman who leaves her abusive husband, experiences independence, and is pressured to marry once more. Highly regarded by feminist scholars today, Haywood was a prolific writer who revolutionized the English novel while raising a family, running a pamphlet shop in Covent Gardens, and pursuing a career as an actress and writer for some of London's most prominent theaters.

# A Note from the Publisher

Spanning many genres, from non-fiction essays to literature classics to children's books and lyric poetry, Mint Edition books showcase the master works of our time in a modern new package. The text is freshly typeset, is clean and easy to read, and features a new note about the author in each volume. Many books also include exclusive new introductory material. Every book boasts a striking new cover, which makes it as appropriate for collecting as it is for gift giving. Mint Edition books are only printed when a reader orders them, so natural resources are not wasted. We're proud that our books are never manufactured in exce
quantity they need to be read and enjoyed.

# Discover more of your favorite classics with Bookfinity™.

- Track your reading with custom book lists.
- Get great book recommendations for your personalized Reader Type.
- Add reviews for your favorite books.
- AND MUCH MORE!

Visit **bookfinity.com** and take the fun Reader Type quiz to get started.

Enjoy our classic and modern companion pairings!

## Classic & Modern